'It wouldn't work,' Shelly insisted in an irritated voice.

'I'd rather pay a childminder to look after Matthew. At least that way I'd know they were doing things properly.'

'Properly!' Ross repeated her last word through pursed lips.

'Yes, properly, Ross,' Shelly snapped, her words coming out way too harsh. But suddenly Ross was getting too near for comfort, making promises he would surely never, ever keep, and—perhaps more to the point—Shelly was terrified of letting him into her life. Terrified that one look at the real Shelly, the mum, the housewife, the eternal juggling game that her life was at the moment, would have Ross scuttling away in two seconds flat.

But Ross wasn't ready to even consider taking no for an option!

Carol Marinelli did her nursing training in England and then worked for a number of years in Casualty. A holiday romance while backpacking led to her marriage and emigration to Australia. Eight years and three children later, the romance continues… Today she considers both England and Australia her home. The sudden death of her father prompted a reappraisal of her life's goals and inspired her to tackle romance-writing seriously.

Carol now also writes for Modern Romance™!

Recent titles by the same author:

Medical Romance™

THE ELUSIVE CONSULTANT
THE SURGEON'S GIFT
EMERGENCY AT BAYSIDE
ACCIDENTAL REUNION

Modern Romance™

THE BILLIONAIRE'S CONTRACT BRIDE

THE BABY EMERGENCY

BY
CAROL MARINELLI

First published in Great Britain 2003
Large Print edition 2004
Harlequin Mills & Boon Limited,
Eton House, 18-24 Paradise Road,
Richmond, Surrey TW9 1SR

ISBN 0 263 18149 9

Set in Times Roman 16½ on 18 pt.
17-0504-46875

Printed and bound in Great Britain
by Antony Rowe Ltd, Chippenham, Wiltshire

PROLOGUE

THERE were two very good reasons Shelly didn't want to be there.

For one thing, the barrage of sympathetic stares and awkward greetings that were sure to greet her she could certainly do without.

And as to the other…

Darting into the changing room, she rather unceremoniously dumped the mud cake she had bought on the bench, before checking her reflection in the full-length mirror.

The pregnancy books had been right about one thing at least—the mid-trimester glow they had promised as a reward for the constant nausea and mood swings had finally appeared.

Glowing was the only word that would describe her.

Even Shelly, with her eternally self-critical eye, acknowledged that for once in her thirty years her skin was smooth and clear with not a blemish in sight. Even her long auburn curls seemed to be behaving for the first time in memory, falling in heavy silky tendrils instead of their usual chaotic frizz, and her vivid green eyes were definitely sparkling.

Funny she should look so good when everything around her was falling apart.

Closing her eyes, Shelly took a deep cleansing breath, trying to settle the flurry of butterflies dancing in her stomach. Even the baby seemed to sense her nervousness, wriggling and kicking, little feet or hands making certain they were felt.

'It's OK, baby.' Shelly put a protective hand to her stomach and spoke softly, hoping her falsely calm voice might somehow soothe the child within. 'We're going to face this together.'

Touching up her lipstick, Shelly fiddled with her top for a moment, the flimsy powder-blue top softening the ripe bulge of her stomach. She even indulged for a tiny moment the still surprising sight of a cleavage on her increasingly unfamiliar body.

This should be such a happy time. The words buzzed around in her head. How she wanted it to be happy, how she wanted to enjoy the changes that were overwhelming her, to be afforded again the luxury of revelling in what had been a very much planned and wanted baby.

Still wanted.

A fresh batch of tears was adding to the sparkle in her eyes and, blowing her nose loudly, Shelly practised a forced smile in the mirror and picked up the cake. Looking down at her bump, her free hand went back for a final comforting stroke of the baby within. 'Come on, little one, let's get this over with.'

'Shelly!' Her name seemed to be coming at her from all directions as her colleagues welcomed her warmly, welcoming her straight into the click of things, but despite the smiles and casual chit-chat, not one of them managed to look her in the eye.

Not one of them asked how her pregnancy was progressing.

Except Melissa.

The playroom on the children's ward was for once void of patients and anxious parents, filled instead with staff, some in uniform, some like Shelly in regular clothes, all clutching cups and paper plates, all there to say goodbye to a certain doctor who in his six-month rotation had brought more vitality and energy to the ward than most did in their whole careers.

Like a radar homing in, Shelly made her way over to her staunchly loyal colleague, grateful in advance for the quiet support Melissa in her own unique way would impart. 'Quite a spread,' Shelly said, handing Melissa her cake. 'Anyone would think it was one of the consultants leaving, not a temporary intern.'

'I know,' Melissa sighed. 'Ross can't believe it himself. I think he expected a cake and a couple of bottles of warm cola, but just look at the turn-out! People like Ross don't come along everyday, though. We're all going to miss him.'

And there was Shelly's second reason.

She didn't want to say goodbye.

Again.

Didn't want Ross Bodey, who'd breezed into her life at various intervals over the years, to breeze out again. Didn't want the smile that had brightened her day, the funny chats and sometimes serious insights to end.

It wasn't as if she was alone. Not one person in this room wanted him to go. Ross in his own easygoing, light-hearted way had turned the ward around. Even Tania, the rigid unit manager, had somehow loosened up under his good-natured teasing. Everyone here today was going to miss him.

Especially Shelly.

Over the years they'd grown close.

Very close.

Oh, nothing to be ashamed about. They'd been friends for ages. Shelly had met him first when she'd been doing her midwifery training and Ross had been but a lowly second-year medical student.

The occasional coffee in the canteen had been a welcome interlude, listening as Ross had planned his travels, determined to fit the most into his summer semester break, happy too to let Shelly chatter on as she'd planned her engagement party.

Friends, nothing else.

The five-year age gap between them seemingly unfillable. Ross ready to party, Shelly ready to settle down.

Even when Ross had breezed back this time, ready to resume their friendship, Shelly hadn't had a qualm of guilt. There was nothing in their friendship that threatened her marriage. There was a bond between them, that was all: something special that gelled them. They didn't keep in touch or anything, their friendship only extended to the workplace, but it was their unique bond that made Ross call for her when he needed a hand, that made Shelly ring him first if there was a sick child she wanted seen. OK, maybe she did check the doctors' roster with more than a faint interest these days, and maybe she had put up her hand for a couple of extra shifts when Ross had been on, but there was no harm in that, there was nothing wrong in a man and woman being friends.

Ross was twenty-five years old, for goodness' sake, into nightclubs and trendy clothes. A world away from Shelly's contented suburban existence: happily married, excitingly anticipating the birth of her first child.

Till now.

'Fancy coming out for a drink at the weekend?' Melissa's invitation was casual enough but it was loaded with caring and Shelly bit back the sting of tears.

'I might just take you up on that.'

Dear Melissa. For all Shelly's friends, for all the colleagues who had squealed with delight when they had found out she was pregnant, who had beguiled her with horror stories of their own pregnancies and labour, Melissa, fifty, single and childless, had been the only one to call her up again and again when she had been permanently greeted by the answering-machine. The only one who had ignored Shelly's frosty response and had pressed on regardless.

When friends were being doled out, Melissa had been a treasured find.

'Shelly!'

Finally a pair of eyes were actually managing to look at her.

Very blue eyes, almost navy in fact; the dark lashes that framed them a contrast to the blond hair flopping perfectly and no doubt intentionally onto his good-looking face.

'Hi, Ross.' The forced smile was still in place and Shelly widened it an inch. 'Given that it's your last day, are you going to finally admit that you do dye your hair?'

'Never.' Ross grinned. 'How would I find the time for all that palaver with roots and regrowth? You're just going to have to accept that I'm naturally good-looking, isn't that right, Melissa?'

'No comment.' Melissa shrugged good-naturedly then she let out a deep throaty laugh. 'Who am I trying to kid? You're stunning, Dr Bodey, you know it and so does everyone else. Just don't let it get to your head.'

Waddling off, she left an open-mouthed Shelly gaping in her wake. 'I do believe Melissa was flirting.'

'Terrifying, wasn't it?' Ross winked.

The smile she had been forcing was coming more naturally now and Shelly took the plastic cup he'd brought over for her and took a quick sip of some very questionable cola.

'Thanks for coming, by the way. I know you're on days off.'

'As if I wouldn't have said goodbye. What are you doing tonight, having a big family send-off?'

'Hardly.' He gave a quick shrug and for the tiniest instant Shelly could have sworn she registered the beginning of a frown, but it soon faded, the nonchalant smile she was so used to soon back in place. 'They're used to me wandering off by now. It'll just be a case of too many beers with a few choice friends. Come if you want.'

In Shelly's present mood, Ross's invitation didn't even merit a response and Shelly didn't bother to try.

'Come on,' Ross pushed. 'I'll even shout you a cola, with ice,' he added, grimacing as he took another sip.

'It's better I don't, I'm not exactly in the mood for a party. Anyway, we're going to the tennis tonight.'

'You lucky thing,' Ross exclaimed. 'It's the quarter-finals too. I've been trying to get tickets all week—how did you manage to swing that?'

'I didn't,' Shelly sighed. 'We're going with Neil's work, another boring night making small-talk. Still, at least I can distract myself looking at the players. Who knows? Maybe one of them will see me sitting there in the stands and fall head over heels then whisk me away from all this.' She caught his quick grin. 'I'm allowed to fantasise, aren't I?'

'Of course,' Ross said, that quick grin splitting his face now. 'But given that it's the women's quarter-finals tonight, Shelly, that particular fantasy of yours is doing terrible things to my blood pressure!'

'Ross!' Shelly exclaimed, the first laugh she had expended in days spilling out of her lips as she blushed a rather unbecoming shade of claret and quickly changed the subject. 'So, are you all packed?'

'No.' He shrugged as Shelly's eyes widened.

'But you're going tomorrow.'

'So? I'll pack in the morning. I don't think I'll need much in the middle of the outback, a few shorts and T-shirts, a pair of boots. No doubt you'd have had checklists as long as your arm, trying to cram everything into ten suitcases.'

'Probably,' Shelly admitted with a begrudging smile. 'I just like to be—'

'Prepared,' Ross finished with a laugh. 'Super Nurse Shelly Weaver, prepared for any eventuality.'

'Not quite.' The smile was fading now and Shelly took a sip of her drink, eternally grateful to Ross for bringing it over, glad for something to do with her hands.

'Did you find out what the sex of the baby is, then? Or are you going to keep us all in suspense?'

'Sorry?' Shelly looked up, startled, sure she must have misheard him.

'You said were going to find out what you were having when you had your scan. Come on, you can tell me. I'm leaving so it won't get out.' He was still smiling, his grin so broad and his face so innocent Shelly truly thought he couldn't have heard the news.

'I found out a bit more than the sex.' Shelly took another long drink, wiping away her cola moustache with the back of her hand as Ross just stood there patiently waiting for her to explain. 'The scan showed up some anomalies,' Shelly continued, her voice faltering every now and then as she spoke. 'And after further tests the upshot is that I'm going to have a Down's syndrome baby, or a special needs child, or whatever the latest buzz word is for it at the moment.' Her green eyes shot up to his and the tears that were always appallingly close these days sparkled as they brimmed, ready to splash onto her cheeks. The bitter note in her voice was so out of place in her normal sunny nature even Shelly looked shocked at the venom in her voice. 'I'm surprised you hadn't heard already. News normally spreads like wildfire around here.'

'Melissa told me,' Ross said simply. 'I'm sorry for what you're going through. How are you managing?'

'Fine,' Shelly said through gritted teeth. 'It's not as if I have any choice *but* to manage.'

'And Neil?' Ross probed, ignoring her obvious desire to end the conversation.

'Not so fine.' Suddenly her paper cup was coming under intense scrutiny as Shelly fiddled with it in her hands. 'Neil likes to be in control, likes to have choices, a say in things. He's having trouble taking in the fact that no amount of second opinions or dollar-waving is going to change the outcome of this pregnancy.'

'But he's supporting you?'

Shelly gave a very short, very brittle laugh. 'Is that what you call it?' As soon as the words were out Shelly wished she could somehow erase them. Moaning about Neil, no matter how merited, no matter what the circumstances, seemed wrong somehow, but Ross didn't seem fazed by her outburst. Instead he pulled the shredded cup from her hand, his eyes never leaving her face.

'I shouldn't have said that,' Shelly mumbled as Ross stood there patiently, waiting for her to elaborate.

'Why not?' Ross asked simply, when no explanation was given.

'I just shouldn't have said anything, that's all.' She was almost biting through her lip in an effort to keep the tears back, and had the exit door not been located on the other side of the room Shelly would have turned and left there and then. She hadn't come here for this. A quick goodbye was all she'd intended, and now here she was on the verge of letting five days of tortured anxiety burst forth and blubbering like an idiot in front of everyone.

'Oh, Shelly, I'm sorry.' His voice was suddenly serious, the tone directly hitting the final straw of Shelly's reserves. As one large tear rolled onto her cheek a strong arm pulled around her thickened waist as he gently led her out of the playroom and into a small annexe where they stood alone and for the first time in days Shelly felt free to let the emotions she had held in check so painfully finally flow as Ross's gentle voice gently gave her permission to continue. 'Talk to me, Shelly. I know I'm going, but it doesn't mean I don't care. I know there's nothing I can say, but I can listen.'

'There's nothing anyone can say. I'm sick of seeing the pity in people's eyes, sick of everyone adding up how many weeks pregnant I am in their heads and wondering if it's too late for me to have a termination. It's my baby.' Tears were streaming unchecked now. 'It's my baby and I don't want to get rid of him. So he's not going to perfect! It doesn't mean I don't want him. I should still be allowed to love him.'

'It's a boy, then?'

His words were so calm it stilled her, and as she looked up Shelly saw that he was smiling.

'Congratulations.'

'You mean that?'

'Of course I do, Shelly. You're going to have a beautiful little boy and you're going to be a fabulous mum. Yes, he's going to have some problems, need some extra care, but if ever there was a woman who could give a child that then it's you. It might all seem a jumble now, but you'll work it out.'

'Do you really think so?'

'I don't think so,' Ross said emphatically. 'I know so. You and Neil will deal with this.'

'What I said before, about Neil, I mean. I was just letting off a bit of steam. He's upset, which is understandable. It's hard for him too. All the dreams he had, *we* had, have just suddenly gone.' She gave a small laugh, trying to lighten the loaded silence around them. 'I think Neil had our baby pegged to be Prime Minister one day.'

'What's the population of Australia?'

Shelly had no idea where he was leading, no idea where he'd plucked that question from, but her mind whirred away from her problems for a millisecond as she struggled with her appalling general knowledge. 'About twenty million, at least I think that's what it is.'

'The odds weren't great, then.'

Shelly's forehead creased as she tried to fathom where Ross was leading. 'What on earth are you going on about?'

'If you factor in the rising population, increased immigration, well, suffice it to say…' His hand moved forward, gently reaching the soft swell of her stomach as Shelly stood smiling at his strange logic. 'This baby was never going to be Prime Minster. But you can still have dreams for him, Shelly, still cherish his life.' His hand was still there, she could feel the warmth spreading through her top. The baby was motionless, perhaps feeling the quiet confidence Ross so effortlessly imparted. If only over the awful past few days she had endured Neil could have said just one of the comforting words Ross had conveyed so easily,

'You'd better get back.' Her voice was strangely thick. All she wanted to do was lay her head on that chest, feel those strong arms around her, for just an ounce of his strength to somehow rub off on her. 'And I've got to go.'

'Not yet,' Ross moaned. 'I'll get stuck with Tania. If you think Melissa was bad, just wait till you see how Tania's behaving. I swear she's wearing lipstick. I think she's got a crush on me.'

'She has.' Shelly laughed. 'So watch yourself.' Pulling her bag over her shoulder, Shelly swallowed hard. 'I really do have to go. I just popped in to say goodbye. I've got an appointment with Dr Forbes at two.'

'I thought Dr Lim was your obstetrician.'

'He is. This visit is for Neil. I know it's not going to change anything, but he just wants another opinion.'

'Come on, I'll walk you out to your car and say hi to Neil. It would be nice for us both to put names to faces and maybe I can answer some of his questions. His mind must be working overtime.'

'Neil's at work.' She saw a hint of a frown mar Ross's near-perfect features and instantly jumped on the defensive. 'He can't take an afternoon off work every time I see a doctor, he'd never get anything done.'

'Of course not.'

There was a tiny awkward moment as Shelly turned to go. What should she do, shake his hand? A casual wave as she got to the door? Ross answered the question before it had even formed in her mind. Pulling her towards him, he held her for a moment, her bump pressing against his toned abdomen, until he moved away just enough to place his hand on her swollen stomach. 'Look after that mum of yours,' Ross whispered to the babe beneath his hand. 'She's one in a million.'

A tiny kiss was aimed at her cheek but Shelly moved nervously, his lips grazing hers for less than a second, but it felt as if they were both moving in slow motion, every tiny movement magnified, the soft warmth of his mouth on hers as unexpected as it was welcome, and Shelley swallowed hard as he pulled away, biting back tears as he squeezed her shoulder in one final supportive gesture and then he was gone. Off to his party, off on his travels again, off to the outback to impart and absorb, a million miles away from Chisholm Hospital, from the beach and the world he'd become so much a part of in the six months he'd been back.

Her lips were burning from his briefest touch and Shelly shook her head as she walked, her speed increasing as she pushed the unwelcome stirrings from her mind.

Of course Ross Bodey was going to say the right thing, he was a doctor, for heaven's sake! He'd just spent the last six months on a children's ward, dealing with anxious parents and sick kids. Of course he knew how to handle her, that was his job. She was being unfair, comparing his reaction to Neil's.

Neil was the one living it. Neil was the one whose life had changed for ever when they'd found out the news.

Still…

Starting her car, Shelly pulled off the handbrake and indicated to turn right, gliding into the afternoon traffic as she headed for her doctor's appointment, for an afternoon of scans and blood tests, an afternoon of being prodded and poked in a futile attempt to obtain a different version. A little piece of news that might brighten Neil's day. But no amounts of scans, no amount of technology or statistics were going to change the outcome. Their baby was handicapped, and no amount of wishing was going to change that fact.

But she could still have dreams for him.

Ross's words washed over her, a soothing interlude in an awful day. And in the weeks and months that followed they comforted her with increasing regularity, a life raft to cling to in the turbulent times that followed.

She could still have dreams for her son.

CHAPTER ONE

'SORRY, darling.' Marlene put down her basket on the hall floor and haphazardly deposited a kiss on Shelly's cheek. 'The match went on for ever.'

Shelly gave her mother an easy smile to show there was no harm done. 'I've got plenty of time before my shift starts. Is Dad still there?'

'Of course,' Marlene replied crisply, with a slight edge to her voice. 'This twilight tennis competition is supposed to be a combined effort for the two of us to get fit, yet your father undoes all of the hard work in one fell swoop. He's in the clubhouse guzzling beers and eating lamingtons as I speak. Goodness, Shelly,' Marlene said, finally looking at her daughter properly for the first time since she'd arrived. 'You look nice—very nice, in fact! What have you done to your hair?'

'I just put a bit of mousse in it in when I washed it,' Shelly answered vaguely as Marlene gave her a rather sceptical look.

'I'll have to try some. Where's Matthew?'

'Asleep.' Shelly rolled her eyes. 'At long last. But I think this new routine is finally starting to work. I gave him his bath at seven, read his blessed book five times and now he's out like a light.'

'Oh, really?' Marlene's face broke into a wide grin and she gestured behind Shelly. 'So who's this, then?'

'Matthew,' Shelly wailed. 'You're supposed to be asleep.'

Holding up his dog-eared book, Matthew's podgy little face broke into a wide and very engaging smile, instantly dousing Shelly's irritation. '*Wun, wun,*' he begged.

'No more run, run,' Shelly corrected, smiling despite herself. 'The little gingerbread man is fast asleep now and so should you be.'

'*Wun, wun.*' Matthew insisted, his grin widening as he saw Marlene. 'Nanny.'

'Yes, darling.' Marlene scooped her grandson into her arms. 'Nanny's looking after you tonight while Mummy goes to work.' Marlene pulled Matthew closer, whispering loudly in his ear so that Shelly could hear. 'Or at least that's where she says she's going, but I've never seen Mummy looking quite so stunning for a shift on the children's ward!'

'Mum,' Shelly moaned. 'Don't talk like that—you'll confuse him.'

'I'm just teasing,' Marlene soothed, turning her attention back to Matthew. 'Now, give Mummy a big kiss goodnight and we'll wave goodbye to her, then how about we go and see if there's any nice biscuits in the cupboard?'

'Mum.' Shelly's voice had a warning note to it which Marlene dismissed with a wave of her hand.

'The biscuits are for me, darling. Why should your father be the only one ruining his waistline? I'm going to have a nice cuppa then I'll read Matthew his story. You go off to work. Don't worry about us two, we'll be fine.'

'I know,' Shelly admitted, giving Marlene a quick kiss before lingering a while longer with Matthew's. 'Love you, Matthew.' He smelt of baby soap and lotion and as she kissed him gently Shelly wondered, not for the first time, how she could bear to go to work and leave him. Reluctantly Shelly picked up her bag and, turning in the doorway, she forced a cheerful wave. 'If one of those biscuits does happen to find its way to Matthew…'

'I know,' Marlene sighed. 'Make sure I brush his teeth.' Holding up one of Matthew's hands, she guided him into a wave as Shelly opened the car door, the tempting scent of a neighbour's barbeque wafting over the fence. Even though it was nudging eight-thirty, it was still so light Shelly wouldn't even need to put on her headlights, and it would have been so tempting not to go, to curl up on the sofa with Matthew and read him his beloved book.

Not that Matthew would thank her for it, Shelly mused as she turned onto the freeway and headed towards the hospital, Matthew would be having the time of his little life right now, gorging on biscuits and dancing around the lounge with his eccentric grandmother, who would end in one night the routine Shelly had been so painfully attempting to implement.

'Who are you trying to kid?' Shelly mumbled, rallying slightly as she caught sight of herself in the rear-view mirror, her pale eyelashes gone for ever, or at least the next couple of months, thanks to this afternoon's tint. As tempting as a cuddle on the sofa with Matthew might be, tonight, for the first time in ages, she couldn't wait to get to work. Putting her foot down slightly, Shelly felt a tremble of excitement somewhere in the pit of her stomach as the signs for the hospital loomed ever closer, the brightly lit building coming into view, the hub of staff outside Emergency indicating something serious was on its way in. A security guard indicated for Shelly to clear the entrance road. Pulling over, she sat in her car patiently waiting as an ambulance flew past, its flashing blue lights adding to the theatre of it all, watching as the emergency staff leapt forward to greet it. Shelly felt the bubble of excitement in her stomach rapidly expand.

Chisholm Hospital had never looked so exciting!

'Thank goodness you're on tonight, Shelly.' Melissa patted the seat beside her at the nurses' station. 'I've had agency staff with me every night this week—it will be nice to have someone who actually knows the place.'

'You smell nice.' Turning, she smiled at Shelly who sat blushing as red as her hair. 'You look lovely too—been to the hairdressers?'

'No,' Shelly lied. 'You're just used to seeing me coming on an early shift at seven in the morning.'

'Hmm.' Melissa looked at her knowingly but didn't push further. 'So, how many nights are you down for?'

'You're stuck with me for a month.' Shelly rolled her eyes. 'I've been avoiding it for ages so it had to catch up with me sooner or later. Tania rang me at home this morning and told me you were tearing your hair out.'

'I was and I know it's probably the last thing you need right now, but I for one am glad you said yes to a stint on nights.'

'I really didn't have any choice.' Shelly shrugged. 'There's been a big fat zero beside my name where night shifts have been concerned recently. Bring back the old days, I can't stand internal rotation.'

'Sounds painful!'

Shelly let out a gurgle of laughter and stood up delightedly. 'Ross!'

'The one and only.'

'Only you could find a sexual connotation with the nursing roster! So how are you finding it? Back in civilisation after all this time?'

'I've had a very civilised couple of years, thank you very much,' Ross corrected, wagging his finger playfully. 'There's a bit more to the outback than tents and billy tea but, yes, it's good to be back, I think.'

'You think?' Shelly questioned with a grin. 'I would have thought they'd be treating you gently on your first day back.' She was blushing to her toenails now, shamefully aware that the perfume, the hairdresser's, even the shaved legs and smooth bikini line had been done entirely for the benefit of this quick delicious moment at handover, to show Ross somehow that she hadn't completely let herself go just because she'd had a baby. There was nothing like an old friend reappearing after a prolonged absence to force a critical look in the mirror, and now that the vague chance she'd catch Ross on his way off duty had materialised, Shelly was taken back by the rush of emotion that had engulfed her.

Ross Bodey was back in town, and he looked absolutely divine, his blond hair practically white now, courtesy of the hot Australian sun, and his face brown and smooth, accentuating the impossibly blue eyes.

'I've only just set foot in the place.' Ross grimaced. 'Luke Martin is off sick so they rang me at the crack of dawn this morning to tell me I'm going to be stuck on nights for the next week, so there goes my social life. How about you?'

For a second Shelly's eyes flickered to Melissa who sat innocently staring at the whiteboard, jotting down the names of the children and babies under the care of the ward that night. 'I don't have a social life, Ross. I've got a son to think of now. Wine bars and night-clubs are but a distant memory these days.'

'I meant what shift are you on?'

'Nights.' Shelly had to forcibly remove the grin from her face and remember she was supposed to be disgruntled about the fact.

'So we're stuck with each other?' Ross wasn't even pretending to look disgruntled. He was grinning from ear to ear, teasing her with his smile.

'It looks that way.'

'So you don't have a social life.' Smiling, he tutted a few times. 'Haven't you heard of babysitters?'

'Not with the tantrums my son's been throwing lately. I wouldn't inflict that temper on anyone just yet.'

Ross just laughed. 'So Matthew's hitting the terrible twos with a vengeance?'

'That's an understatement.' Shelly's voice stayed light, her grin stayed put, but her mind was whirring as the beginning of a frown puckered her forehead. 'How did you know his name?'

Ross shrugged. 'Melissa told me. So who's looking after him tonight?'

Her frown deepened. Melissa had obviously told Ross a bit more than Matthew's name.

'My parents are, they've been really good. You know about Neil and me, then?'

Ross nodded. Moving away from the desk slightly, they found their own private space in the corridor, slipping so easily back into their ways of old. 'It can't have been easy for you.'

Shelly gave a slightly brittle laugh. 'That's an understatement.'

Ross didn't comment at first, the silence around them building as Shelly stood there wondering how much to tell, scuffing the highly polished floor with her rubber soles and leaving little black marks that would have the cleaners in hysterics in the morning.

'Neil told me he was leaving us the day I was due to be discharged from hospital, the day I was supposed to bring Matthew home.' Her voice was shaky and she couldn't even look up as she recounted her story, sure the inevitable pity she was so tired of seeing in people's eyes would send her into floods of tears. 'He said he couldn't cope with a handicapped child, that it just wasn't what he was cut out for.'

'Then you're better off without him.'

Shelly looked up with a start. There was no pity in his voice or in his gorgeous blue eyes, just the cool sound of reason.

'So everyone keeps telling me,' Shelly sighed. 'And they're all probably right. But is it better for Matthew? Surely he needs a father?'

'Not that sort,' Ross said quickly, his voice strangely flip, a defiant jut to his chin. Suddenly he looked older than twenty-seven. He certainly didn't look like the carefree backpacker she'd built in her mind. He looked every bit the man he was. 'Children need to feel loved, safe and wanted, which are the three things Neil can't give him, so if you ask me, Matthew's better off without him. You, too, so I'm not going to make small-talk, passing on my condolences about the demise of your marriage when your divorce obviously agrees with you. You look the happiest I've seen you in a long time.'

'I am,' Shelly said slowly, the words a revelation even to herself. The divorce had hurt, but her grief had been expended long ago. The tears she cried now when she thought about the end of her marriage weren't for herself and what she'd lost but for her little boy, a two-year-old child whose father simply didn't want to know. Yet for all the angst, for all the struggle, both financially and emotionally, for all the responsibility of being a single parent, for the first time in over two years Shelly actually realised just how much she had moved on.

That she was finally making it.

Not happy exactly, but definitely getting there.

As Melissa stood up Shelly picked up her notepad. 'I'd better go and get the handover. I'll catch up with you later.'

'No doubt about that.'

Her cheeks were burning as she took handover, her mind flitting as she desperately tried to concentrate, tried to ask intelligent questions and make sure she had all the drip rates and drugs due diligently written down in her usual neat handwriting as Annie, the sister in charge of the late shift, told the night staff about the patients on the ward. But there was no chance of that. Her mind was saturated with Ross, going over and over their brief but long-awaited exchange. Still, when Annie gave the details of the latest admission, Shelly's ears pricked up and all thought of Ross flew out of the window, momentarily at least.

'We've got a new patient direct from Theatre—Angus Marshall, twenty months old with a spiral fracture of the femur.'

Shelly's eyes shot up as Annie continued. A spiral fracture in a child was an injury that sounded alarm bells and Shelly's were ringing, but Annie quickly shook her head to dispel any worries.

'The staff in Emergency are happy with the story—they don't think it's a non-accidental injury. Apparently he's just started walking so the injury could have happened when he fell.'

'Could have?' Shelly questioned, knowing that injuries like that were sometimes caused by an abusive parent.

'They're not sure how it happened, there's a big sister and a new baby at home so it's obviously a busy house. Apparently Angus was very grouchy and reluctant to weight-bear and his mum noticed the swelling so she took him to their GP who sent them over to us.

They're nice people, the child's beautifully looked after.'

'That doesn't mean anything.' Melissa's stern voice matched Shelly's thoughts exactly.

'I'm going on what I've been told. They've been interviewed extensively by Dr Khan down in Emergency and he's satisfied that it was a simple accident, so it's not up to us to go jumping to conclusions.'

'Nobody's jumping,' Shelly said in a calm voice, trying to diffuse the undercurrents. 'But with an injury like that, child abuse has to be considered.'

'Which it has been,' Annie answered stiffly. 'And it's been discounted.'

'So, how many beds does that leave us with?' Shelly asked when she realised the discussion was going nowhere.

'One bed and two cots,' Annie said, closing the folder she was reading from. 'But Emergency just rang and they're probably going to be sending up a three-month-old boy with bronchiolitis, which will leave you with just the one cot.'

'Probably?' Shelly checked.

'He's quite sick, they're still deciding whether or not to transfer him to the Children's Hospital in case he needs an ICU cot as our intensive-care beds are all taken. Ross is just heading off down there to see him.'

'Well, I hope Ross takes into account there's only three night staff on and Nicola's only a grad,' Melissa said with a warning note to her voice that had Annie again ducking for cover. Melissa was a straight talker and didn't care who got hurt along the way. Feelings didn't come in to it when she was dealing with her beloved babies. 'It's not like on days where staff are falling over themselves. One critical baby is bad enough but there's a couple more here that could go downhill quickly.'

'Ross knows all that,' Annie said defensively. 'But this baby has been down in Emergency for eighteen hours now, and there's hardly a paediatric intensive care cot left in Melbourne, so someone's going to have to take him. Anyway, Emergency just had a big multi-trauma come in and they need to start moving some of the patients.'

'Well, maybe you should have thought of that earlier,' Melissa carried on, without even blinking. 'You know as well as I do that we're going to get this baby. He should have been admitted and settled by now while there were enough staff to do it comfortably, not left till Emergency's bursting at the seams and there's no choice but to move him.' And without another word she headed out onto the ward, leaving the rest of the staff chewing their lips and rolling their eyes.

'Good luck with her tonight,' Annie said with a grimace. 'She's in a right old mood.'

'I don't blame her,' Shelly said quickly, and to the other staff's obvious surprise. 'That baby should have been admitted ages ago, not just left for the night staff.'

Minor bickers like this were uncomfortable but commonplace on a busy ward. Even though Shelly hadn't done a stint on nights for ages she knew how busy it was, and also knew that as much fun as Annie was to work with she was also very good at putting things off for the next shift to deal with. Melissa had been right to say something and Shelly was only too happy in this instance to defend her. As the day staff departed Shelly gave a comforting smile to a nervous-looking Nicola.

'When Melissa said you were "only a grad" she wasn't aiming it at you personally, just pointing out the staff levels,' Shelly said, moving straight to the point.

'I know that. It's just that she seems so fierce. I know I haven't worked with Melissa but I've seen her in handover and it's enough to put anyone off. I've been dreading coming on nights.'

'You haven't worked with Melissa yet,' Shelly pointed out. 'You've only seen her in here. She's nothing like that out there.' Shelly gestured to the ward and gave Shelly a reassuring smile. 'Any bad feeling stays in the handover room, that's an important rule on the children's ward. The patients pick up on bad vibes otherwise. Anyway Melissa's as soft as butter really. Once the day staff are gone you'll see that for yourself. As fierce as she can be, Melissa's also the best nurse here, you can learn a lot from her. There's nothing about sick children Melissa doesn't know. She's been doing this job for more than thirty years now, so if there's anything you're worried about don't sit on it, just tell her, OK?'

'OK.' Nicola nodded but Shelly could see the poor girl was still terrified.

'It will be fine, you'll see.'

It *was* fine. The obs and drug round went smoothly. Even the raucous older children, some bored from weeks in traction, seemed fairly settled, exhausted from too many visitors and computer games and a day spent good-naturedly teasing the nurses.

Melissa was in charge so she worked both sides, overseeing all the patients and keeping a watchful eye on Nicola as she settled the children and did the late round. Shelly took the cots, which consisted of eight airy rooms all surrounded by glass, which meant at any given time she had an uninterrupted view of her patients but they were all effectively isolated so as not to spread any infections. Six were occupied and Shelly checked each child carefully, smiling to herself as she did so, taking in the little bottoms sticking up in the air, thumbs tucked into mouths, the babies sleeping on blissfully as Shelly watched over them. A couple of the cheekier babies had extensions on their cots to stop them climbing out, but for now they all looked like cute little angels.

Angus was sleeping and Shelly roused him gently, carefully checking his observations and the little toes sticking out of the damp plaster, making sure the circulation to his foot was adequate. Annie was right, Shelly thought as she flicked on the cot light and checked him more closely, Angus *was* beautifully kept—his little nails short and clean, his hair soft and shiny, no rashes or bruises, nothing to indicate he was anything other than loved and cherished.

'Is he all right?' Mrs Marshall's anxious face appeared at the end of the cot. 'I was just getting a coffee.'

'He's fine,' Shelly reassured her. 'He'll probably sleep soundly for the next couple of hours. He was given a strong painkiller so he's quite comfortable. Would you like me to get you a camp bed? We can set it up beside the cot.'

Mrs Marshall shook her head. 'Thanks, but no. The day nurse, Annie I think her name was, already offered, but I'm going to go home. I've got the other two to sort out and it's been an exhausting day.'

'I'm sure it has. We can always ring you if there are any problems, if he gets too distressed,' Shelly said.

'Of course.' Mrs Marshall gave a tired smile. 'But he normally sleeps right through.' The mobile telephone ringing in her bag made them both jump and Shelly waited patiently as Mrs Marshall took the call.

'That was my husband, Doug. He's come to pick me up.' Walking over to her son, she gave him a tender kiss and stroked his little lock of hair. Shelly knew she should mention that mobiles were supposed to be turned off on the ward, given her little lecture about the interference they could cause with the equipment, but she didn't. Trying to put herself in Mrs Marshall's place for a moment, she figured it could wait for the morning.

Shelly had always been a quick worker and was grateful for the chance to make up a few bottles for when the babies inevitably awoke and to prepare some jugs of boiled water and change the sterilising solutions. Happy she was on top of things, Shelly set up an oxygen tent for the inevitable new admission and prepared the sterilising equipment and nurses' gowns along with some literature on bronchiolitis for the undoubtedly anxious parents.

'How's it going?' Melissa popped her head in the darkened room and smiled as she saw Shelly setting up the room. 'Finally, someone who doesn't have to be told! How are they all?'

'Settled. I've put the new admission in here so it's nearer the nurses' station, but cot six needs an eye kept on—she's still a bit wheezy even after her nebuliser. Cots two and four are due for a feed at eleven so I've left their obs till then. Their mums aren't staying, so if they wake up at the same time I might need you or Nicola to feed one of them—their bottles are all ready.'

'Good.'

'How's Angus?'

'Fine.'

'And the mother?'

'She's fine too, she's gone home.'

Melissa shot her a shrewd look. 'So what's the problem?'

'I don't know,' Shelly admitted. 'I know lots of mums go home, that it doesn't mean anything at all...'

'Just that you wouldn't?'

'I've only got one child.' Shelly flicked her eyes down to her handover notes. 'Mrs Marshall's got three and one of them is a young baby. She might be breastfeeding so it's totally understandable that she had to go home.'

'So why aren't you convinced?'

Shelly shrugged. 'Her husband rang her from the ambulance bay. Surely he'd want to pop up and see Angus and say goodnight?'

'Maybe he's got the other two asleep in the back of the car,' Melissa pointed out. 'Imagine if Security found two children unattended in the car park. The social workers would have a field day!'

Melissa was right, of course. There was a perfectly reasonable explanation and Shelly gave her head a small shake, determined to concentrate on the facts. But she'd misjudged Melissa, the conversation wasn't over yet.

'Just keep your eyes and ears open. I'm not entirely happy myself.' For a moment their gazes lingered on the sleeping toddler, both women deep in their own thoughts for a moment. 'Come and have a cuppa before they wake up,' Melissa said finally with forced cheerfulness. 'I'll go and put the kettle on.'

'Sounds marvellous.'

'Wait till you taste the cake I've made. Ross is already champing at the bit.'

'Melissa?' Shelly called as Melissa made her way out of the ward. 'Just what did you say to Ross exactly?'

'That I'd baked a cake!' Melissa gave Shelly a quizzical look as if she'd gone completely mad!

'I'm not talking about the cake, Melissa.' Shelly took a deep breath. She didn't want to ruffle any feathers but the fact Melissa had taken it on herself to tell Ross so much about Shelly's personal life needed addressing—the very last thing she needed was Melissa playing Cupid. Ross Bodey had enough women after him without thinking he had Shelly on his list of swooning fans. 'Ross knows Matthew's name, he seems to know all about the divorce, I just wondered how.'

'I might have said something...' Melissa shrugged.

'You mean you gave him a life update on me the second he entered the ward. Why?'

'I didn't,' Melissa said quickly. 'I hadn't laid eyes on Ross until I saw him when I was with you, honestly,' she insisted as Shelly gave her a disbelieving look. 'Believe it or not, as riveting as your life might seem to you, it's not my favourite topic of conversation. Ross and I have kept in touch while he's been away, I probably said a few things then in passing.'

'Oh.' Thankfully the room was in semi-darkness and Melissa couldn't see the blush flaming on her cheeks, but with the heat it was radiating Shelly was sure she must be able to feel it winging its way across the quiet room.

'He's rung a few times at night when he's needed something looked up or wanted a bit of advice on a patient. He's a good doctor is Ross, not too up himself to ask a nurse for advice, and when he rang we'd have a chat. He'd ask what the gossip was, who was seeing who, who was pregnant, who was leaving, that type of thing. We didn't just talk about you, Shelly.'

Suitably chastised, Shelly wished the ground would swallow her up whole.

'I'm sorry,' she mumbled. 'I was just taken back that he knew so much about everything.'

'That's Ross for you.' Melissa shrugged. 'You know he loves all the gossip.'

'Sure.' Fiddling with the oxygen tubes, Shelly kept her voice even. 'Go on, then, get the kettle on, I'll finish up in here.'

Once alone, Shelly sank onto the camp bed she had made up for the baby's mother. Sitting perched on the end, she buried her burning cheeks in her hand, trying for the life of her to fathom why Ross keeping in touch with Melissa had upset her. Why was she feeling like a jealous schoolgirl all of a sudden?

'Blast,' she muttered, then flicked her eyes open to check the coast was still clear. As if Ross would be that interested in her marriage problems. As if Melissa was going to rush to fill him in on the latest saga.

She really wasn't that important.

It had just been a casual chat, a snippet of gossip Melissa had imparted to a bored doctor stuck in the middle of nowhere, eager for a chat, happy to while away the lonely hours on call with an old friend. She should have been relieved, relieved that Melissa hadn't embarrassed her, that she hadn't bent his ear about the divorce with a nudge and a wink and a load of innuendo.

But…

The green-eyed monster was rearing its ugly head again.

Why hadn't Ross rung her? Why had he kept in touch with Melissa over the last few years?

And why did it matter so much?

'Damn,' Shelly said more strongly, the words whistling through her gritted teeth as she forced herself to take a deep steadying breath as realisation finally hit.

The hairdresser's, the perfume, the long overdue meeting with her razor hadn't been a coincidence. Hadn't even been a vague attempt to show an old friend she hadn't completely let herself go.

Of all the stupid things to go and do…

Of all the ridiculous, ludicrous things she had done in her time, this one certainly took the biscuit.

Developing a king-size crush on a certain Ross Bodey was the last thing Shelly needed to deal with. Her cheeks scorched with embarrassment at the thought of him finding out, that the dependable, organised Shelly, his on-duty friend and confidante, had succumbed like legions of others to his blue-eyed charm.

He was miles out of her league, young free and single, not just a world away but an entire galaxy from Shelly's routine existence, and it would serve her well to remember the fact.

Ross Bodey was way out of bounds.

CHAPTER TWO

PULLING up a chair at the nurses' station, Shelly smiled at a now much happier Nicola.

'She's great, isn't she?' Nicola said, happily munching into a huge slab of walnut cake.

'Told you. Melissa's bark is far worse than her bite. Once the day staff are gone she relaxes—and feeds us,' Shelly added, helping herself to a generous slice.

'Save some for me!' Ross perched on the edge of the desk, depositing a mountain of files and X-rays as he did so.

'How's the baby in Emergency?'

'Heading this way,' Ross sighed. 'He's pretty sick but he's holding his own at the moment. The children's hospital has got an ICU cot but not a general one, whereas we've got a general but no ICU. I can't believe I'd managed to forget the constant battle with the bed state.' He rolled his eyes. 'Looks like we're in for a long night. Hopefully Melissa will go easy on me, I didn't really have any choice but to admit him. Emergency's steaming down there, it's no place for a sick baby.'

'I agree.' Melissa, coming up behind Ross, caused him to jump. 'I don't mind being busy, Ross, it's just the general thoughtlessness that annoys me. Annie should have had him up here hours ago. Instead, we've got a sick baby to assess and an overwrought mum to deal with in the middle of the night. A little bit of foresight wouldn't have gone amiss.'

Ross nodded his head in agreement. 'Right, what have you got for me? I'd better clear the pile before Kane gets here. Who knows when I'll find time otherwise?'

'Just a couple of IV orders that need updating, and I think Shelly wants some antibiotics written up for cot five—his blood culture results are back.'

Ross nodded. 'Yeah, the lab just paged me.' One hand tapped away on the computer as he brought up the results. 'This is the life,' he sighed. 'Pathologists on call, X-Ray just a stone's throw away.'

'I thought you said it was civilised where you were,' Shelly teased, desperately trying to resume normal services despite her internal bombshell.

'It was. The clinic I worked in at Tennagarrah was comparable to a luxury caravan. All the basics were there but you weren't exactly spoilt for choice and you had to work for everything. This in comparison is a five-star hotel.' With an exaggerated whoop of delight he jumped down and opened the drug fridge. 'And just look at the mini-bar, where do I start? Bactrim, flucloxacillin, gentamicin, vancomycin. What can I get you, Sister?'

Shelly peered at the monitor in front of her, reading the blood results and the antibiotic sensitivities. 'Well, a large dose of flucloxacillin would hit the spot.'

'Coming right up.

'Anything else I can get you?' Ross asked, carrying on the joke as he pulled the vial of antibiotic out of the fridge. 'Have you had a look at the room service menu yet?'

'This will do just fine.' Picking up her cake, Shelly effectively ended the playful conversation. Images of five-star hotels and bubbling spas and four-poster beds weren't exactly doing wonders for her blood pressure, and the sight of the porter wheeling in the gurney carrying the baby provided a very welcome diversion.

'Kane Anderson,' the emergency nurse informed them as Shelly pulled down the cot side and greeted Kane's mum with a warm smile. 'He's been down in Emergency so long he's part of the furniture now. This is his mum, Angela.'

'Hi, Angela, we're just going to get Kane into the cot and then I'll get the handover from Emergency. Once that's done I'll come and settle you both in.' Gently she lifted the infant over, handling him deftly and with minimum fuss so as to avoid any unnecessary exertion.

Although the handover was important and the emergency nurse was obviously in a rush to get back to her department, Shelly took a moment or two to explain how the oxygen tent worked, realising how alarming it must look to Angela.

'This monitor tells us the oxygen concentration in the tent, it's very safe.'

'He can't suffocate?' Angela checked.

'Definitely not,' Shelly said firmly. 'If the level drops in the tent the alarm goes off, and this little probe I've attached to his foot tells us Kane's own oxygen levels. I'll be back in a couple of moments. I'm just outside but if you're worried at all just bang on the window or call.'

'She's being a bit difficult,' the emergency nurse started.

'No doubt because she's worried and exhausted,' Shelly said quickly, refusing to get drawn into a discussion on the mother's emotional state, preferring to make her own observations. 'And eighteen hours in Emergency wouldn't exactly have helped matters. What's the story with the baby?'

The story wasn't very good. Three days of a worsening cough and struggling to feed, two different types of antibiotics from the local GP and a long wait in Emergency. 'His respiration rate is still very high and his heart rate's elevated. He's very grizzly, which isn't helping his breathing, and he just won't settle.'

'Any wet nappies?' Shelly asked, flicking through the obs chart.

'Three. He was moderately dehydrated when he came to us but the IV fluids have kicked in now. He's still very sick, though.'

Shelly nodded in agreement. Her brief assessment of Kane had done nothing to reassure her. He was working hard with each rapid breath, using his stomach muscles, his tiny nostrils flaring, all dangerous signs. 'I'll get Ross to have another look at him,' Shelly concluded, anxious to get back to her small charge. 'Thanks for that.'

Ross was already at the cot side, rubbing his stethoscope between his hands to warm it before placing it gently on the baby's rapidly moving chest as Angela stood anxiously wringing her hands, every bleep of the monitors making her jump slightly, every tiny jerking movement Kane made causing her to step forward anxiously, bombarding Ross with questions as he tried to listen to the baby's breathing.

'He's hungry,' Angela said the second Shelly entered. 'The sister in Emergency said he might be able to have a bottle once he got up to the ward.'

Pulling the stethoscope out of his ears, Ross straightened, carefully zipping up the oxygen tent and pulling up the cot side. 'He can't have a bottle at the moment, Angela, he's too exhausted to feed.'

'But he isn't settling.'

Shelly could hear the slightly hysterical note creeping into Angela's voice and stood back quietly as she carried on with her outburst.

'They said they were going to put a tube down his nose and give him the milk that way, but they haven't even done that. No one seems to be doing anything. He's not even on any antibiotics!'

'Look, why don't you sit down for a minute?' Ross started, but his well-meant words only inflamed Angela further.

'I don't want to sit down,' she shouted. 'I want someone to tell me what's being done for my baby.'

'I know you're upset—' Shelly started.

'Oh, what would you know?' Angela snapped, turning her fury on Shelly, her face livid.

'That you're exhausted, and terrified?' Shelly ventured, her stance relaxed, her voice calm and sympathetic. 'That you've probably had more people offering their opinions and telling you what might be, could be, should be done than you can even count?'

Mistrusting eyes finally made contact and Angela gave a grudging nod.

'Well, you're on the children's ward now, and Ross is the doctor and Melissa and I are the nurses looking after you and your son tonight. If you'll let us, we can tell you what we're going to be doing, but shouting and getting upset is only going to unsettle Kane—can you see that?'

The nod Angela gave wasn't so grudging this time, more sheepish, and Shelly felt her heart go out to the other woman as she burst into noisy tears. 'I'm sorry, it's not you, I'm just so scared, he keeps getting worse.'

'He's been sick for a few days, hasn't he?' Shelly asked gently.

'Since the weekend. I thought it was just a cold at first then he got this cough and then he started wheezing. I haven't slept for the last two nights.'

'Kane has bronchiolitis,' Ross broke in, gently taking Angela's arm and guiding her to a chair before pulling one up for himself. 'It's a respiratory virus that can be particularity nasty in young babies. Now, because it's a virus antibiotics aren't going to do any good, none at all,' he emphasised as Angela opened her mouth to argue. 'What Kane needs at the moment is what we call supportive care. That means he needs to be kept warm and rested, with lots of oxygen to help him breathe and fluids through a drip to keep him hydrated. All of this we're doing for him, and this in turn gives his body a chance to concentrate on fighting the virus. If we give him a bottle now he wouldn't be able to cope with it, he simply hasn't got enough energy to feed. If we give him one at this stage he could become a very sick little boy indeed.'

'What about the tube they were talking about?' Angela asked hopefully, her mind still focussed on her baby getting fed, but Ross firmly shook his head.

'The tube we would pass is very small and fine, but it would still upset him while we passed it and I don't want to cause him any more distress, that's why I'm going to try and not to do any blood tests or anything that might upset him, for now we just want him to rest. Kane's getting what he needs from the drip and we can give him a dummy to settle him.'

'He keeps spitting it out.' Angela's voice was rising again, her shredded nerves ready to snap at any moment, but Ross carried on chatting, his voice amicable and easy.

'We can soon fix that.'

'How?' Angela snapped.

'Glycerine.' Ross gave an easy shrug as Angela immediately shook her head.

'You're not supposed to put anything on their dummies, it says so in all the books. The child health nurse said—'

'Kane's very sick,' Ross interrupted gently. 'He needs to rest, and if a smear of glycerine on his dummy achieves that, then it's merited.'

'Ross.' Shelly gave him a wide-eyed look and Ross frowned slightly at the interruption. 'Can I have a quick word, please?'

'What's up, Shelly?' Following her outside, there was a slight impatience to Ross's stance. 'I'm trying to calm the mother. Pulling me outside isn't really helping.'

'I know that,' Shelly responded. 'But putting anything on the babies' dummies really is frowned on. Tania will have a fit…'

'Tania isn't here,' Ross pointed out. 'And if she was I'd tell her what I'm about to tell you. That baby's sick—any further slide in his condition and he'll be on a ventilator in intensive care. Now, given this hospital hasn't even got an intensive-care cot, that will mean sending him and Angela for a ten-minute jaunt in a helicopter. Now, if a bit of glycerine on a dummy can prevent that, I'm all for it.'

'But, Ross.' Shelly pulled at his sleeve as he turned to go, the contact tiny but enough to throw her, the sleeve of his white coat new and crisp, the solid bulge of his forearm, even the scent of his aftershave wafting over as he turned to go, all enough to distract her. Shelly fumbled to finish her argument.

'I know it seems petty, but the department has strict guidelines on this. The dental damage—'

'Shelly.' Ross's voice was quiet, but his words were very clear as he spoke, his eyes looking right into hers, unblinking, unwavering. 'Let's get this little guy through tonight, huh? Lose this battle and tooth decay will be something Angela can only dream about.'

Shelly's eyes were wide with surprise as Ross turned and went back to Kane. His words made sense, good sense, and in truth Shelly felt ridiculous arguing about such a tiny detail, but rules were rules... But it wasn't Ross's little lecture that had left her reeling.

The few years in the bush had changed him. That easygoing, eager-to-please guy was gone, and in his place, just as gorgeous, just as stunning, was a rather more confident version, a man who knew what he wanted, and would make sure he got it.

Heading to the treatment room, Shelly took a while to find the little-used jar.

'The contraband's arrived,' Ross said dryly as Shelly joined him at the bedside, Angela looking on anxiously, still dubious that it would work.

'It's just while he's sick,' Shelly said confidently, noting the tiny smile of appreciation on the edge of Ross's lips as she put aside her own misgivings and beckoned for Angela to come closer. 'What's more, it's something *you* can do for Kane to help him settle.'

Her words hit the mark. As Angela took the dummy, Shelly went into greater detail, showing Angela how to open the tent, how she could slip her hands in and even put her head in the cot to cuddle and speak to her child. Thankfully the glycerine worked and after a few goes baby Kane finally took his dummy. With the tent delivering a high dose of concentrated oxygen, he lay back exhausted, his little arms and legs flopping outwards like a washed-up frog as he drifted into a spent sleep.

'How's he doing?' Melissa's knowledgeable eyes scanned the monitors and baby in a moment.

'He's asleep, his saturations are ninety-two on thirty-five per cent oxygen.'

'Turn it up to forty per cent,' Melissa said after a moment's thought. 'Let's give him as much help as we can.'

Ross nodded his approval as Shelly fiddled with the flow meter.

'Come and have a cup of coffee,' Melissa offered to Angela.

'I'd rather not leave him. Can I have it in here?'

'Sorry, but the last thing you or the staff will be thinking of if Kane gets worse suddenly is a hot cup of coffee balanced on the locker.'

'Fair enough.' Angela was positively meek now, but even Shelly thought Ross was pushing things with what he said next.

'Go and have a coffee.' Ross's voice was assured. 'And then come back and have a lie-down.'

'I'm not sleeping,' Angela flared. 'How can I sleep when he's this sick? What if he gets worse?'

'He probably is going to get a bit worse.' Ross's eyes held Angela's terrified ones. 'And then he's going to start getting better, and when he does he's going to have you running in circles, feeding him, amusing him, spoiling him rotten...' He gave a tiny smile and to Shelly's amazement Angela gave a reluctant one back. 'You need some rest, you need to try and trust us to look after your baby, and you're going to be right next to him.' He gestured to the camp bed, his eyes never leaving Angela's face. 'And if anything happens, we'll wake you.

'I promise,' he added.

'You've got the A team on tonight,' Melissa broke in, her brisk, efficient voice such a contrast to Ross's calm one, but somehow the balance worked. 'Your baby's in good hands. Now, come and have a coffee with me while we go through the admission forms. I need to know his little ways, what formula he has, how you generally settle him, that type of thing.' Technically the job was Shelly's, she was looking after cots tonight so the admission was hers, but Shelly was more than happy to defer to Melissa. They were a team and Melissa was what Angela needed right now—someone a touch more authoritative, less close in age, someone to lean on.

'She'll be right now,' Ross said quietly as Melissa led Angela out. 'That's why I wanted to just get them up here. The poor woman was beside herself down in Emergency. A slice of Melissa's cake and a bit of a rest and she'll be a new woman.'

He was right, of course. Ross was always right when it came to dealing with women, Shelly mused, fiddling again with the flow meter to get the concentration right now that the cot was zipped up and Kane was quietly resting. Someone must have given Ross a glimpse of the rule book the day he hit puberty, told him how to turn on that winning smile and work that velvet voice to gain maximum impact. Oh, he wasn't a flirt, he didn't turn on the charm to beguile people, it was all just so damned effortless with him and it would be so, so easy to let it go to her head.

To forget that the smile she was privy to right at this very second was the same gorgeous smile he used on everyone.

Even Kane.

'Cute, isn't he?' Ross murmured. 'I love fat babies.'

Shelly gave a little laugh at his simple description, her eyes taking in the sleeping infant as a woman for a moment, not as a nurse. 'Matthew was like that.' Her voice was soft, her mind dancing backwards, remembering him soft and warm in her arms, that delicious baby smell filling her nostrils, Matthew's dark curls soft and warm against her arm as she'd held him close and nursed him. 'The child health nurse even had to tell me to cut down on his feeds he got so big.'

'A little Buddha?'

'That's what I used to call him.' Shelly looked up with a start then righted herself. It was hardly an original nickname. 'He's nothing like that now, though, he's the fussiest eater in the world.'

'Unless it's ice cream?' Ross caught her eye as she gave a small nod. 'I'd love to see him.'

'I've got some pictures in my bag,' Shelly said lightly. 'I'll get them out when we've got a moment.'

'I meant I'd like to meet him.' Suddenly the tension was palpable, his eyes not moving, taking in every flicker of her startled reaction. 'See for myself if he's as cute as his mum.'

'Flatterer.' Shelly shrugged off his compliment with a smile and picked up the obs charts, which really didn't need filling in just yet. Holding his gaze would just have been too hard. 'Anyway, he's a bit tricky with strangers.'

She wanted this to be over, didn't want Ross working his winning ways on her, didn't want their friendship moving out of the safe confines of the ward, terrified her cool façade might slip and he'd register the shift in her feelings. But Ross simply refused to take the hint, whipping the safety net from under her with one stroke of his silver tongue and sending Shelly into freefall.

'That's easily solved.' His words were slow and measured but the effect was instantaneous. Shelly's heart rate surely matching the monitor bleeping rapidly beside her as Ross plunged her world into confusion. 'Don't let me be a stranger, then, Shelly.' Wrapping his stethoscope around his neck, he gave her a tiny questioning smile as she stood there, trying to think of something to say, eternally grateful when Melissa appeared with a very groggy Angela and the awful loaded silence was broken.

'One exhausted mum,' Melissa fussed, tucking in the sheets around Angela as she climbed gratefully into the camp bed, 'and one sleeping baby.'

'You'll wake me,' Angela checked as Melissa flicked off the main ward light, leaving only the cot-side lamp on, and gestured for them all to leave.

'Of course we'll wake you,' Melissa said assuredly. 'Ross promised, didn't he? And, believe it or not, you're looking at a guy who actually keeps his word.'

CHAPTER THREE

'WHAT'S the problem?' His eyes bleary from sleep, his blond hair anything but immaculate, Ross huddled into his white coat and yawned loudly as he took a seat next to Shelly at the nurses' station.

'No problem,' Shelly said, barely looking up, concentrating instead on getting Angus to finish the training cup filled with milk that she was trying to get into him. 'Why?'

'My pager just went off.' Pulling it out of his pocket, he peered at it closely. 'Or at least I thought it did. I woke up with the most terrible fright.'

'You were dreaming.' Shelly laughed. 'I thought you'd have grown out of that by now.'

'I wish,' Ross muttered. 'Every time I've got a really sick one it's the same. I lie there half-asleep waiting for my pager to go off, and when it doesn't I wake up with a jump thinking I've slept through something.'

'Well, you didn't,' Shelly said matter-of-factly. 'Kane's still sleeping.'

'Any better?' Ross asked hopefully, but Shelly shook her head.

'Not really, that's why I'm feeding Angus up here at the desk, so I can keep an eye on him. Nicola's on her break and Melissa's in room five with a child having a nightmare.'

'Must be the night for it,' Ross muttered, glancing at his watch. 'Five a.m. already. It's not even worth going back to bed—I'll never get back to sleep now.'

A loud angry wail made its way down the corridor and Shelly let out a moan. 'Well, if you're not going back to bed, make yourself useful and go and put cot four's dummy back in for me—she's been keeping me running all night.'

'Sounds like she wants a bit more than a dummy,' Ross yawned as he stood up.

'Tell Tayla she'll just have to be patient. Her bottle's warming and as soon as I've finished this little one, she'll get her turn.

'And wash your hands first,' Shelly reminded him as he wandered off. 'Hey, little guy.' Tickling Angus under his chin, Shelly attempted to raise a smile, but his solemn eyes wouldn't meet hers. 'You really wanted that milk, didn't you?'

'What are you doing?' Shelly grinned, looking up from Angus as Ross wandered back, dressed in a white nurse's gown and holding an angry pink bundle in one hand and pushing a portable bassinet with the other.

'What female knows how to be patient?' Ross asked good-naturedly, settling himself in the chair and holding out the bottle. 'Check the temperature for me.' He shook a few drops onto her wrist and when Shelly nodded he balanced the baby on his knee and attempted to offer her the bottle, which Tayla promptly spat out, her wails of protest increasing.

'You need to cuddle her in.'

'In what?' Ross asked, bouncing her up and down on his knee as Tayla's cries gained in momentum.

'Into your chest. Wrap her up more tightly in the blanket and hold her against you.' She watched, fighting the urge to put her own patient down and interfere as Ross clumsily wrapped the baby up, leaving her little pink feet kicking in the air. Ever meticulous, Shelly liked things neat and organised but baby Tayla didn't seem to mind Ross's haphazard methods, her cries instantly stopping as one blond-haired arm wrapped firmly around her and pulled her in close.

Lucky little thing, Shelly thought reluctantly.

'It worked.' Ross grinned. 'She likes it.'

'For now,' Shelly warned briskly. 'But that good mood won't last long if you don't follow it up with her bottle.'

Ross did as he was told and soon Tayla was guzzling, batting her little blue eyes at her enthralled admirer and somehow managing to coo and drink at the same time.

'Another female you've won over,' Shelly said dryly.

'If only they were all so easy.' Looking over, he gave Shelly a slow smile. 'It's like having twins, isn't it?'

'Heaven forbid,' Shelly said lightly, deliberately shooing away the rather cosy little images fluttering into her mind. The beginning of a shadow was dusting his chin, his eyes blinking with tiredness as he stifled regular yawns, and he looked so completely adorable Shelly felt like joining Tayla and cooing in blatant admiration.

Sure, the odd doctor had in his time given a baby a bottle at night, and sitting at the nurses' station nicking biscuits and cake was an annoyingly regular occurrence, but it was the *way* Ross did things. His absolute delight in the simple things in life made moments like these precious, made sitting feeding two little imps at five o'clock in the morning on a hushed children's ward so special it almost brought a lump to Shelly's throat.

Ross looked over as Shelly pulled Angus in for a cuddle.

'How's he doing?'

'Good. He's had all his milk, he hasn't made a murmur all night.'

'Has he had any paracetamol?'

'He hasn't needed anything,' Shelly said lightly, but her voice trailed off as she saw a frown pucker Ross's face.

'Give him some anyway.' Ross's voice was suddenly thick, a serious look Shelly had never yet witnessed marring his normally happy face. 'Maybe he's in pain and has just given up complaining about it.'

'You think he's been abused as well?' Shelly looked down at the dozing child in her arms and her heart ripped another inch. 'But Dr Khan seems to think—'

'Forget what Dr Khan "seems to think",' Ross interrupted bitterly. 'Look at him, Shelly, look at him. Why isn't he cooing like Tayla? Why isn't he smiling or even crying come to that? Why isn't he asking for his mum?'

There was such a raw note to his voice, such an edge of urgency that Shelly looked up from Angus, startled. Never had she seen Ross like this. Sure, he was a caring and compassionate doctor; sure, he got upset at times, they all did, but something in his voice told Shelly that Angus had touched a nerve, a raw painful nerve, and Shelly was momentarily at a loss as to how she should react.

'Ross…' she started, but he shook his head.

'Leave it, Shelly.' He took a deep breath and looked back down at Tayla. 'Please.'

Which pretty much ended the conversation.

Standing, Shelly held Angus closer as she found his prescription chart from her neat pile on the desk and opened the drug cupboard, measuring out the medicine with one hand, a feat she had mastered to perfection after so many years on the children's ward.

Angus took the syrup without a murmur of protest, but instead of putting him back into his cot, Shelly sat back down. In the scheme of things one extra cuddle wouldn't make much difference, but it surely couldn't hurt!

'So how was your first night back?'

'Not the best.' Ross shrugged, his usual smile noticeably absent. 'Nothing changes here, does it?'

'Of course not,' Shelly quipped. 'Why change the habits of a lifetime?' Still Ross didn't smile, and Shelly felt her own smile fading as Ross continued.

'After I left here I had to go over to the postnatal ward and check the lab results on a baby with jaundice. She needs to go under the phototherapy lights and when I told the mum she started crying because she doesn't want her baby in the nursery away from her for the next thirty-six hours.'

'It happens all the time, Ross,' Shelly said lightly. 'Why on earth would that upset you?'

'Because it's so unnecessary. I suggested to the midwife we move the lights into the mother's room, she's in a side ward, the equipment wouldn't bother anyone else…'

'What did the midwife say?'

'She agreed with me,' Ross sighed. 'Trouble is, she's been having the same running argument for the last three years and hasn't got anywhere, because policy dictates that phototherapy takes place in the nursery. Apparently if we make allowances for one, all the mums will be demanding side wards if their babies need the treatment.'

Shelly sat deep in thought for a moment, her first instinct to sigh and agree with Ross, the pettiness of hospital protocol achingly familiar, and yet…

Green eyes darted upwards and suddenly Shelly felt defensive, longing to reassure him, for Ross to feel as enamoured of the place as she did, because if he didn't…

The alternative was too awful to contemplate.

'Doesn't it ever get to you?' Ross asked, breaking into her thoughts.

'Sometimes,' Shelly admitted. 'But it's a big hospital, Ross, there's always going to be a policy that irks if you go looking for it. I just try not to let it get to me. I enjoy my work on the children's ward, I do my job to the best of my ability and then I go home, that's enough for me.'

'Is it?' Ross questioned, and Shelly took another moment as she pondered his question.

'It has to be, Ross. I've got a mortgage, a child to think of. I can't go around demanding changes, questioning the wisdom behind every decision. Sure, sometimes I get frustrated, sometimes I'd like to be able to do my own thing, but in a hospital this size it's just not going to happen.'

'It would in Tennagarrah.'

Shelly heard the shift in his voice, the slightly wistful note as he moved in his chair and smiled down at Tayla.

'You really miss it, don't you?' She watched the slight nod of his head then ventured further. 'If you loved it so much, how come you came back?'

'I had my reasons.' His eyes found hers then, but they didn't dart away, didn't turn back to a contented Tayla or relax into a smile. Instead, he held her gaze, not blinking or wavering as Shelly felt her colour deepen, felt the weight of his stare and the dearth of unanswered questions behind it.

Confused, self-conscious under his scrutiny, Shelly broke the moment, tore her eyes away and looked down at Angus who was sleeping peacefully now. 'Let's get you to bed, little guy.'

Angus's room was quiet and Shelly lingered a moment as she tucked him in, brushing the blond curls back from his face and placing one of the hospital's teddy bears under the blanket beside him.

But it wasn't just Angus keeping her there. Suddenly she was strangely reluctant to go back outside without the easy diversion of feeding a baby, unnerved by the blatant openness of Ross's stare. But there was a pile of notes waiting to be written, and hiding in a cubicle wasn't going to get them done!

'I didn't know you wore glasses.' Ross grinned as Shelly opened a folder and started her nursing notes, relieved at the shift in tempo. 'When did that happen?'

'Sometime after I hit thirty,' Shelly said grimly, her forehead creasing as she concentrated on the paperwork.

'They suit you.'

His observation went without comment as Shelly worked diligently away, Kane's history too important to be sidetracked by small-talk.

'Talk to me, Shelly,' Ross grumbled as she worked on in silence.

'I'm working.'

'So am I,' Ross responded, placing a sleeping Tayla into the bassinet beside him. 'Come on, Shelly, talk to me. I haven't seen you in well over two years.'

'You're worse than Matthew,' Shelly sighed. 'At least *he* can amuse himself for five minutes. Look, I'm busy right now, Ross. Make yourself useful and put the kettle on.'

Which took him two seconds flat.

He really was worse than Matthew, leaning over her shoulder when she wrote, correcting her spelling and generally buzzing around like an annoying fly. A gorgeous diversion he might be at times, but right now a diversion wasn't what Shelly wanted or needed!

'Can I see the photos?'

'What photos?'

'The ones you said you had in your bag.'

'They're in my purse,' Shelly mumbled, chewing on her pen and gesturing to the bag, but Ross just sat there, annoyingly close, his blue eyes boring into her rapidly darkening cheeks. 'What now?'

'I can't just go through your bag. You'll have to get them for me.'

'You really are annoying, Ross, do you know that?' Kicking the bag in his general direction, Shelly pointedly turned back to her notes. 'I promise there's nothing exciting in there. If there is, we'll halve it.'

But for all her nonchalance, for all her supposed annoyance, as Shelly sat there, writing, her heart was in her mouth as she focussed on the blur of words in front of her, struggling with an overwhelming desire to turn her head to see Ross's reaction when he saw Matthew for the first time, though why it should matter, why his opinion should count for much, Shelly truly couldn't fathom.

'He's beautiful, Shelly.' Ross's voice was quiet and there was a difference she couldn't pin down, a subtle shift from the observations he had so readily imparted about Kane and Tayla. She acknowledged him then. Turning, she caught her breath as he took in the pictures, his eyes scanning each shot, a flickering smile lighting up his tired face.

'He's just gorgeous.'

She waited, but the words she silently dreaded didn't materialise, didn't impinge on the moment. No ifs or buts, no sighs or if onlys.

Ross in his own sweet way had said the three little words Shelly really needed to hear.

CHAPTER FOUR

'HOW was your night, sweetheart?' Marlene flicked on the kettle the second a weary Shelly pushed open the front door.

'Busy,' Shelly answered, a huge smile splitting her tired face as a pyjama-clad bundle dived off the couch and ran the length of the hallway. 'Hi, Matthew.' Her instinct was to scoop her son into her arms and kiss the Vegemite-streaked face but, ever mindful of bringing germs home from work, Shelly settled instead for a quick kiss on the cheek. 'Just let Mummy have a quick shower, darling, and I'll be with you in a moment.

'Two minutes,' she added to Marlene, before darting into the bathroom and taking the quickest shower in history and dressing at lightning speed.

Everything seemed to be done at lightning speed these days.

Work, crèche runs, cooking, cleaning, even mothering.

'How was he?' Running a comb through her long auburn curls, Shelly scraped her hair into a scrunchy before taking a grateful sip of her coffee.

'Fine. Once he went down, he slept all night.' There was a long pause, which struck Shelly as unusual. Marlene was normally regaling her with tales, not necessarily about Matthew. They could be anything from the movie she'd seen, the newspaper headlines, to what she was cooking for dinner that night—anything other than silence.

'What's wrong, Mum?'

'Nothing.' Marlene's voice didn't sound particularly convincing as she busied herself stacking dishes before turning around, a worried frown out of place in her usual sunny face. 'You know there's a group of our friends going to Fiji on Saturday?'

Shelly nodded. 'That's right. You didn't want to go.'

'We did want to go.' Her voice was wary and Shelly jerked her face up as Marlene continued. 'We just didn't think it would be fair on you.'

'What on earth made you think that?' Shelly wailed. 'Of course you should have gone. I'd have managed.'

'How?'

'Matthew's in crèche now. I'd have worked my shifts around and if not I'd just have taken annual leave. You and Dad do enough for us, you deserve a holiday. I can't believe you'd pass one up without talking to me first.' Shelly was gesturing wildly in the air, the longed-for cup of coffee quickly forgotten as she struggled with what her mother was telling her.

Ken and Marlene had been wonderful.

Wonderful.

When Neil had dropped the bombshell that their marriage was over, Ken and Marlene had put their hands up straight away. Had picked up a shell-shocked mother and her newborn from the hospital as if it had been the most natural thing in the world, and had practically spoon-fed Shelly through those blurry postnatal days until gradually her reserves had strengthened. They'd helped her find a new house, decorating it for her until it had become a home, babysitting endlessly, there at the drop of a hat or a ring of the telephone, sleeping over in Shelly's house when she'd worked nights so as not to disrupt Matthew's routine and generally going way beyond the call of any dutiful parent.

And it was starting to show.

Marlene and Ken were getting older, and co-raising a boisterous toddler, exhausting at the best of times, was a hard feat as they neared their sixties. The endless guilt Shelly felt as she saw her own parents suspend their lives in the name of love surfaced at that moment and she struggled with tears that welled in her eyes.

'Why didn't you talk to me, Mum?'

'I am talking.' Marlene forced a smile. 'June and Roland can't go. She's got to have a little operation, and if she puts it off, heaven knows when her name will come up again. If they back out now, they'll lose all their money…'

'You and dad could take their places,' Shelly said quickly, as Marlene gave a worried nod.

'That's what we were thinking.'

'Do it, Mum. Please.'

'But how on earth will you manage?' Marlene asked hesitantly.

'Like every other single parent!' Shelly exclaimed. 'How long will you be gone?'

'A week,' Marlene said doubtfully.

'I can manage for a week, for goodness' sake!' Shelly exclaimed. 'If you pass this up I'll never forgive myself and I'll be furious with you. I'm furious already that you didn't even discuss it with me the first time around. Look, Matthew's my son, not yours. You and Dad have been wonderful but I don't want you to give up your lives for us. Dad should be enjoying his retirement, not worrying about crèche runs and babysitting duties…'

'We love doing it,' Marlene protested.

'I know that, Mum,' Shelly said wearily. 'And, to be honest, I don't know how I'd have managed without you, but I have to start standing up on my own two feet a bit more, I have to start holding the reins by myself, and a week without you will be a good practice run. When do you have to let June and Roland know by?'

'This morning.'

Shelly deliberately didn't sigh, purposely kept on smiling as the cosy image of her warm bed was pulled from under her. 'Good. You go and tell them yes and I'll drop Matthew at crèche then I'll go and speak to Tania, the unit manager, about my roster.'

'But you're tired. Why don't you just ring her and then go to bed? I can take Matthew to crèche for you.'

'No.' Shelly's voice was firm but kind. 'He doesn't like going there and I know how upset you get when you leave him.'

'It's for the best, though,' Marlene's voice was wary as Shelly blew out her cheeks. 'It *is*, Shelly. You know Neil's not my favourite person in the world, but he did look long and hard into the best crèche for Matthew. If he follows this programme, he might even be able to go to a normal school.'

'With an aide,' Shelly pointed out.

'Still, it would be nice.'

'For who?' Shelly started, then bit her tongue. Matthew's education wasn't on the agenda this morning. 'His crèche is on the way to the hospital, and it really would be better for me to talk to Tania face to face than do it over the telephone. Anyway…' Shelly managed a reassuring grin '…you've got to get to the travel agent.'

'Just give him a kiss and tell him you'll be back at five, Shelly. He'll soon stop crying when you're gone.'

When I've abandoned him, you mean.

Shelly knew Lorna, the childcare worker, meant well. Knew from her own nursing experience that invariably once the parents had gone children quickly settled. But Matthew wasn't in hospital, this wasn't a two-day admission with the mum popping home for a shower and freshen-up. This was a Monday-to-Friday occurrence and it was tearing Shelly to shreds.

Crying in the car park over her steering-wheel was another Monday-to-Friday occurrence.

Matthew should be at home with her, making fairy cakes, or mud cakes in the garden, sleeping in his own bed for his afternoon nap.

She should be working part time for pleasure, not full time to support them.

Bloody Neil and his big-shot ideas.

Turning on the engine, Shelly wiped the back of her damp cheeks with a shaking hand.

Early intervention, integration. Neil relieved his guilt by paying half of the crèche fees and he had the gall to think he was helping. Shelly didn't want intervention—she wanted to care for her own child in her own home. And as for integration!

'Don't get me started,' Shelly muttered to herself.

Why should going to a *normal* school be the ultimate goal? Why should matching his peers in their milestones be the be-all and end-all?

Matthew *was* different, and it would seem Shelly was the only person in the world prepared to accept the fact.

Tania didn't exactly roll on the floor laughing at Shelly's request to yet again juggle the roster, but the incredulous look she imparted as Shelly falteringly outlined her parents' plans pretty much made the message clear.

'I'd love to help,' Tania sighed, running her eyes down the roster, 'but I just don't see how I can.'

'If I can go back onto days for just a week then I could drop Matthew at crèche early. I couldn't do the late shift, though,' Shelly mumbled. 'The crèche is only open until six…' Her voice trailed off as Tania shook her head.

'The whole point of implementing internal rotation was to share the load, and I'm sorry to say this, Shelly, but in your case this simply isn't happening. You can't expect the other staff to keep covering for you—they've got families of their own to worry about.'

Cheeks flaming, Shelly deliberately didn't rise, her parents' holiday enough incentive to force the issue. 'Can I have some annual leave, then?'

'You've used up all your annual leave, Shelly,' Tania pointed out, running her eye along the holiday schedule. 'In actual fact you owe the ward eight hours.'

'Then can I take it as unpaid leave?' Shelly pushed, hating the fact she was reduced to begging, but there really was no other alternative. 'I hate asking, but it's important.'

'It always is with you, Shelly.' Tania sighed as she put down her pen and fixed her junior with a firm stare. 'I'm sorry, but in this instance my hands are tied, there's just no one to cover you. I've just received yet another memo from Admin about cutting back on agency staff.' Her voice had a slightly pained edge. 'Last month it was Matthew's grommets, the month before chickenpox…'

'I know,' Shelly muttered, scuffing the floor. 'We've had a bad run.'

'I have enough trouble accommodating my staff's holiday requests without having to take into account their parents! I need dependable staff, Shelly, this is a children's ward and it has to be run by competent, reliable staff.' Her words were delivered in a relatively calm voice but Shelly felt the sting of them as surely as if she'd been slapped. To date she'd always prided herself on her competence, her organisation and her meticulous attention to detail, and suddenly here she was being told that even that saving grace was being taken from her.

'When you're here, you're wonderful.' Tania added more gently, the evident shock on Shelly's face softening her stance. 'I know you've had a lot of problems, I know you're home life's rather difficult, and it's a credit to you that you manage to leave your problems at the ward door and deliver excellent nursing care, but I can't keep juggling the roster to fit in with your domestic issues.

'I'm sorry,' she added as Shelly stood up and left the office and in her haste to get out of there didn't even attempt to say goodbye.

'Hey, Shelly, I thought you'd be safely tucked up in bed by now!' Ross was grinning, as laid-back as ever, walking alongside her effortlessly even though Shelly was marching briskly, hoping to make it to the car park before she broke down in tears.

'I had to sort out my roster,' Shelly replied, without looking. 'How come you're still here?'

'I wanted to have a word with the boss about Angus.'

His words stopped Shelly in her tracks and she turned abruptly to face him.

'I'm still not happy with the story,' Ross said with a tight shrug. 'Not that my opinion counts for much.'

'They're not going to report it, then.'

'Dr Khan doesn't think there's any need. "Accidents happen" were his exact words.' His voice was flip, but Shelly knew the words that were coming out of his mouth weren't Ross's. 'I've also been delivered a short sharp lecture on my over-zealous nature. Dr Khan seems to think that as I've been stuck in the bush for the last couple of years I'm chafing at the bit to get my hands into some "real" medicine. Hell, if only he knew what I'd dealt with out there. I tell you this much, Shelly, I don't get any kick out of exaggerating things, but there's something going on with Angus, and I'm the only one who can see it.'

'You're not, Ross,' Shelly sighed. 'I'm not happy either. I've written it all up in my notes and I've handed it over…'

'That's all we ever do.' The angry edge to his voice shocked Shelly and for a second the man that stood in front of her seemed so far away from the Ross she knew that Shelly barely recognised him. But almost as soon as the words were out his expression changed, the easy smile was back and the Ross she knew so well was smiling down at her. 'So, did you get it sorted?'

'What?'

'The roster.'

Pulling her bag high on her shoulder, Shelly resumed her angry march. 'No. In fact, I got my own short sharp lecture this morning, except in my case it would seem I'm not zealous enough. Apparently the ward's been making allowances for my lack of dependability, given my "domestic issues", but it would seem the goodwill has run out now.'

A warm hand was on her arm, a hand that was pulling her back, turning her around to face him.

'Tania can be a right cow sometimes. Don't take it personally, Shelly.'

'But it is personal,' Shelly hissed. 'My mum and dad have run themselves ragged looking after Matthew and the one chance they get to go on holiday I can't even take the time off to look after my own son.'

'You'll work something out.'

'How?' Shelly snapped, her exasperation brimming to the surface.

'Because you always do. Come on, Shell, let's go and get some breakfast in the canteen, have a chat and see if we can come up with something. Two heads are better than one.'

'Oh, spare me the proverbs.' Snarling at Ross was the last thing Shelly wanted to be doing, he didn't deserve it, but she was past caring. If he'd just let her go she could get to the car park, and if he didn't, well, Ross would just have to wear the steam she was blowing in all directions.

'Come on,' Ross pushed. 'At least for a coffee.'

'I don't want a drink, Ross, I want to go home and sleep. I've got to come back here tonight.'

'So do I,' Ross pointed out, his laid-back calmness only exacerbating Shelly's volatile mood.

'Yes, but no doubt you'll get up at eight, hop in the shower and pour some boiling water over two-minute noodles then rock across from the doctors' mess around nine.'

'I don't like noodles.'

'I, on the other hand,' Shelly carried on, ignoring his grin, 'will get up at four, pick up my son and then prepare a dubiously delicious but extremely nutritious dinner, packing in as many omega oils as I can along the way to supposedly increase his brain function. Then I'll try to squeeze in an hour of quality time before I bathe him and attempt to have him tucked up in bed before my mum gets over, and then…' Shelly took a deep breath, her angry, tired eyes finally meeting Ross's. 'Then I'll come and start work.'

He stood there for a moment, eyeing her thoughtfully, as Shelly's colour darkened, stunned at the venom of her own outburst, waiting for him to crush her with some cutting remark.

'Was that a no to the coffee, then?' A lazy smile was tugging at the corner of his mouth, and to Shelly's absolute amazement a reluctant smile was wobbling on the edge of hers.

'Yes, it was a no,' she mumbled, scarcely able to believe after her anger only seconds before she was now almost smiling.

'Some other time maybe?'

Shelly nodded. All the fight had gone out of her and she ached, literally ached for her bed, the vented steam leaving her curiously calm.

'Come on.' His lazy arm slung itself around her and for the tiniest second Shelly let herself lean on him. 'I'll walk you to your car.'

Surprisingly, the steering-wheel wasn't privy to a second batch of tears. In fact, idle fingers drummed on it as Shelly drove home, listening to the radio and singing tunelessly.

She didn't even toss and turn as she lay in bed, her mind didn't throb as she tried to fathom the hows and whys of arranging child-care in her parents' absence, she didn't lie there fretting about Matthew and the beastly crèche. Instead, she pulled the curtains closed on the midmorning sun, slipped into the welcomingly cool sheets and closed her eyes with only one sleepy thought on her mind.

Ross was back.

And how good it felt.

* * *

'What's this?'

Shelly shifted in her seat and quickly folded the papers she had been reading in front of her. The last few days had been spent simultaneously assuring Marlene she had everything in hand and panicking at her inability to organise Matthew's childcare.

So desperate was Shelly, she'd even swallowed every last shred of pride and rung Neil, taken the bull by its very reluctant horns and dialled his office. But even before he had stopped huffing and puffing, even before Neil had admitted there was no way his new wife would even consider having Matthew for a week, Shelly had decided that he wasn't going there anyway.

She'd rather pay someone to look after him than expose Matthew to such blatant apathy!

Which was why Ross had found Shelly sitting at the nurses' station engrossed in the pile of brochures the crèche had provided her with, reeling somewhat at the hourly rates. It wasn't just the money that was the problem—the thought of a stranger looking after Matthew in her house at night while she worked was giving Shelly palpitations! Folding up the papers, Shelly pushed them away on the desk before turning her frown on Ross. 'Don't you know that it's rude to read over people's shoulders?'

'No, it isn't.' Ross laughed. 'Maybe for an uptight puritan like you, but as to the rest of us…'

Shelly swung round on her chair, her jaw dropping incredulously. 'That's a bit strong, even from you!'

Ross just shrugged and spooned three sugars into his coffee. 'Possibly,' he conceded with a grin. 'But it got a reaction. Anyway, you can't afford it.'

'Can't afford what?'

'A live-in babysitter.'

This was getting way too personal and Shelly pulled off her glasses, snapping them firmly in their case before heading off towards Kane's room.

'That's right,' Ross called good-naturedly, 'run off, why don't you? One mustn't discuss money or personal problems or any other social taboos.'

'I'm not running off,' Shelly corrected. 'I'm checking on Brody in cot two.'

'You did that ten minutes ago and, anyway, Melissa's just been in.'

Reluctantly Shelly sat back down, her back rigid, her lips disappearing into her face.

'You can't afford it,' Ross said again. 'Because if you had that type of money to burn, you wouldn't be at work in the first place.'

His irritating logic was unfortunately spot on.

'Ring in sick,' he suggested lightly. 'You get two weeks with chickenpox when you work on a children's ward.'

'Oh, very helpful, Ross.' Shelly gave a slow handclap. '"Hi, Tania, I know I sat in your office and begged for unpaid leave, but it really is just a coincidence that I've come down with chickenpox and can't work for a week. Yes, I know Matthew had it a few weeks ago and I didn't catch it then. Funny, that. And I know you think I'm undependable and are probably about to sack me, but can I take this opportunity to assure you that I'm really very reliable?"'

'All right, bad idea,' Ross shrugged. 'How about I babysit for you?'

'You?' Shelly gave a rather undignified sniff.

'I am a doctor,' Ross pointed out. 'Almost a paediatrician even! I can look after Matthew at night while you work, then you can take over in the day, the same as you're doing with your parents now.'

'But you've never even met him.'

'Neither have any of this lot.' Picking up the brochures, Ross flipped them in the wastepaper basket.

'Why on earth would you want to do this?'

'Because I can.' Perching on the desk beside her, he tapped his thigh with a pencil, his leg so close it occasionally brushed Shelly's as he distractedly swung his feet. 'You need help,' he pointed out. 'And I'm only too happy to give it. Mind you, you'll have to feed me a lot. You already know I don't like noodles, but apart from that I'm pretty easy. I'm not very tidy, though.'

'I'd never have guessed.'

'And I'm a morning person. You can't just march home after a hard night at work and demand silence. I like someone to talk to over my breakfast.'

The image of Ross sitting at her breakfast table was doing terrible things to Shelly's concentration.

'It would never work.'

'Why? I've only got a room at the doctors' mess, it would take two minutes to pack my backpack.'

'It wouldn't work,' Shelly insisted in an irritated voice. 'I'd rather pay someone, at least that way I'd know they were doing things properly.'

'Properly!' Ross repeated her last word through pursed lips.

'Yes, properly, Ross,' Shelly snapped, her words coming out way too harsh, but suddenly Ross was getting too near for comfort, making promises he would surely never, ever keep, and perhaps more to the point Shelly was frightened of letting him into her life. Terrified that one look at the real Shelly, the mum, the housewife, the eternal juggling game that her life was at the moment, would have Ross scuttling away in two seconds flat.

Snapping seemed her only option.

'I like things done in a certain way. You'd probably let Matthew stay up half the night chewing on sweets and no doubt then you'd forget to tell him to brush his teeth.'

Ross roared with laughter. 'You've really got an obsession with dental decay, do you know that, Shelly?'

'People would talk.' She shot him a look, knowing exactly what was coming next and keen to get in first. 'And if that makes me an uptight puritan then so be it.'

'Let them talk.' Ross leant across the table, his dark blue eyes dangerously close, very white teeth that he most certainly had brushed glinting at her as she took in his wide sensual mouth. 'Better still, let's give them something to talk about.'

'This is silly.' Standing up, Shelly shook her head. 'I really am going to check on cot two now.'

Brody was fine, better than fine actually. The little boy who had been keeping Shelly on the run with his exacerbation of asthma was sleeping peacefully, his respiration rate finally nearing normal, his heart rhythm settling and his oxygen saturations spot on.

'I think he's turned the corner.' Ross had come up behind her, and they stood there in the darkness for a moment eyeing the baby, sharing a mutual sigh of relief. 'When did he last have a nebuliser?'

Shelly glanced down at her watch. 'An hour and a half ago and it's still holding him.' Pulling her stethoscope out of her pocket, Shelly carefully listened to the sleeping baby's chest. 'Not even a hint of a wheeze.' She smiled, pulling the earpieces out and offering them to Ross. She moved the bulb of the stethoscope as Ross listened, then looked up with a grin.

'Clear as a bell.'

'Which means you can get some sleep now.'

She felt rather than heard him go. Having written Brody's observations down, she pulled a falling blanket around his little shoulders, her cheeks still burning from the conversation only moments before, a frown puckering her forehead as she recalled Ross's offer.

It was all a joke to Ross. His suggestion, how ever well meant, had irritated her.

As if someone like Ross Bodey was going to take a week out of his life to devote to her and Matthew. Sure, he'd maybe even meant it while he'd been sitting there, but it wouldn't last five minutes. He'd probably already forgotten he'd even offered.

Wrong.

Walking out into the corridor, she jumped as a face came out of the shadows.

'Did you forget something?'

'Your address.' She couldn't read his expression in the darkness but for all the world Shelly was sure she heard a note of nervousness in his voice. 'What nights do you need me for?'

'You're really serious about this?' Shelly checked.

'Totally.'

'Sunday through to Wednesday,' Shelly ventured, watching his reaction closely, waiting for him to baulk at the final hurdle. 'Then back again for one night next Saturday.'

'Fine,' Ross said easily. 'I finish my nights on Saturday morning so I'll have a sleep then come for dinner around six. Don't worry,' he rattled on as Shelly opened her mouth to protest. 'I'll bring the food. You won't have to lift a finger. It'll give me some time to get to know the little fellow and on Sunday afternoon I'll come back to stay.'

'Ross, this isn't going to work,' Shelly said quickly, confused at the turn of events, desperate for some breathing space to think things through.

'Yes, it is.'

He sounded so sure, so confident Shelly felt the frown puckering her brow slip away, and after a moment's more hesitation she took the pad he was offering and scribbled her address, which he deposited in his pocket.

'And it is going to work, Shelly.' One warm hand gently cupped her cheek, the small gesture losing all its innocence as her heart went into overdrive. 'Because we're going to make sure of it.'

CHAPTER FIVE

'HONEY, I'm home!'

Shelly stood holding the front door, grinning as Ross barged in armed with white carrier bags wafting delicious smells.

'What on earth are you going on about?'

'I'm practising for our week of domestic bliss.' Kissing her on the cheek, he shot a quick wink at a rather stunned Matthew who was clinging for dear life to Shelly's leg, one curious eye peeping out from behind her far-too-short skirt. 'Can you show me where the kitchen is?'

She should have been nervous!

She had been nervous!

The entire day had been spent in a flurry of cleaning and scrubbing, and not only the house! Her hair had been deep-conditioned, body lotion had been applied, eyebrows plucked and her wardrobe turned up and over as she'd frantically scrabbled for something to wear.

Something terribly casual, of course.

But also absolutely gorgeous.

A mad dash to the shops at four-thirty had for once been a success given that the very short lilac wraparound skirt Shelly had had her eye on all week actually came in her size.

Even Matthew was amazingly clean for six p.m. The usual sticky fingers for once were gleaming, his jammy face washed and wiped as he stood in very trendy clothes, a world away from the grubby overalls he normally wore around the house. Yet now that Ross was here, now that he'd burst in with his usual wacky humour, Shelly wasn't nervous any more, just very, very pleased to see him.

'How was your day at the office?' She kept up the joke as Ross deposited his wares on her kitchen bench.

'Awful, actually.' For a second the easy smile slipped away and Shelly found herself frowning. 'I had a bit of a run-in with Dr Khan this morning before I finished up.'

'What happened?'

'I'll tell you later.' Ross's eyes shifted to Matthew shyly peering around the kitchen door and his face broke back into its usual wide smile.

'What's that smell?' He sniffed the air, screwing up his nose as Matthew watched.

'Tuna casserole,' Shelly answered primly, awkward in her new skirt and panicking that she was showing too much of her pale legs. 'And don't worry, it's not for you—it's Matthew's dinner.'

'Smells terrible,' Ross quipped as Matthew started to giggle.

'It's very tasty actually.'

'If you like tuna casserole! I've bought Thai for us all,' he carried on, banging around opening cupboards and finding plates. 'Now, that really is tasty.'

'For us perhaps, but Matthew won't like it.'

Well, what would she know? She was only his mother after all.

Matthew, as it turned out, loved Thai food—nearly as much as he liked the cola Ross had bought and the ice cream that followed.

Nearly as much as he clearly adored Ross.

'You'll get bored before Matthew does,' Shelly warned as they engaged in a complicated game of peek-a-boo while Shelly stacked the dishwasher. But yet again her son surprised her—it was Matthew who ended the game. Ross, it seemed, would have gone on for hours.

'Bar.'

'Bath,' Shelly translated easily as she came into the living room, smiling at the two of them lying sprawled on the sofa, watching cartoons. Scooping up Matthew, she carried him out, not even mildly surprised when Ross followed her. 'He always has one around this time.'

'He's his mother's son.' Ross grinned as Shelly stood with there with a questioning look on her face, waiting for enlightenment. 'Bath at seven, bed at eight…'

'He likes to have a routine, all children like a routine, it makes them feel secure.'

'Whatever you say, *Sister*.'

Shelly was prickling with indignation as he followed her to the bathroom. Ross could always do this to her, make her feel uptight, like some antiquated old school nurse.

'Look…' Shelly gestured as she put in the plug. 'Not a trace of carbolic soap in sight.'

'I'm teasing,' Ross said easily. 'Still, you'd better show me where the spare toothbrushes are kept.'

'Here.' Pulling open the bathroom cupboard as she ran the water, Shelly caught his incredulous look. 'What have I done now?'

'I was joking.' He laughed. 'Or at least I thought I was. How many toothbrushes have you got in there!'

'The crèche was doing a fundraiser,' Shelly mumbled as he perched on the vanity unit. 'Each family had to sell ten—it was easier just to buy them myself. I haven't got obsessive-compulsive disorder.

'Yet,' she added with a reluctant grin.

And as easily as that, her awkwardness was gone. The days of frantic preparations, the nights wrestling with the wisdom of having Ross as a house guest disappearing like a puff of smoke as she joined him on the vanity. They dangled their feet and watched as Matthew enjoyed his bath the way only two-year-olds could. Squealing with delight at the mountains of frothy bubbles, filling bottles and emptying them over and over until he worked out that hitting the water directly with the palms of his hands could have the adults present ducking for cover. Ross didn't mind, not at all, and by the end of the bath the two of them were only slightly less wet than Matthew.

It was nice having him there, not awkward, not difficult, just nice. Somehow he seemed to know exactly what was needed, what was wanted, and when Matthew was dressed in pale blue pyjamas, his little eyes blinking as he struggled to keep them open, Ross gave the little guy a playful ruffle of his hair and said goodnight, leaving Shelly to settle the over-excited little boy into his bed.

'*Wun, wun.*' Sticking his thumb in his mouth, Matthew pointed to the much-loved book Shelly was holding, but instead of opening it and getting on with the story Shelly decided to test the water.

'Did you like Ross?' Shelly ventured, knowing Matthew wouldn't answer but hoping for some sort of reaction that would indicate his take on things. 'He's a friend of Mummy's,' Shelly pushed, but Matthew had eyes only for his book. 'He's nice, isn't he?' Climbing on the bed beside him, Shelly pulled Matthew into the crook of her arm as she awaited his response, but a little man made out of gingerbread was all Matthew wanted to hear about now.

'*Wun?*' he said again, his voice more insistent as he looked up at Shelly.

'In a minute, darling,' Shelly said gently. 'I just want to explain things to you. Ross is a doctor,' Shelly explained patiently. 'Mummy works with him at the hospital. He's also a friend, a good friend of mine.' She hesitated then, unsure how much information to give. Telling Matthew now might only upset him but, taking a deep breath, Shelly decided to plant the seed. Matthew's reaction would be the litmus test that would invariably make up her mind. 'While Nanny and Grandad are on holiday, Ross is going to look after you while Mummy works.' She forced a reassuring smile at the innocent little face, half expecting him to burst into tears or break into hysterics, but Matthew's thumb stayed firmly *in situ* as his eyes drifted back to the book.

'*Wun, wun,*' Matthew insisted, apparently none the worse for the bombshell that had just been dropped.

As she took over the story Shelly couldn't make up her mind whether she was disappointed or excited. Disappointed because there was no legitimate reason for calling this ridiculous charade off, or excited because it really looked like it was going to finally happen.

'"As fast as you can..."' Shelly intoned, her mind a million miles away from the page in front of her, achingly aware that Ross was waiting for her in the living room, achingly aware that the night had only just started...

'I thought you said that he was tricky with strangers.' Filling two glasses from the wine bottle he'd brought, Ross handed one to Shelly.

'I meant he's tricky with adults.' Shelly grinned as she took a grateful sip of her wine. 'It's no wonder you got on so well.' Sitting down on the couch, she let out an exaggerated sigh. 'I love him to bits, but it's bliss when he finally goes to bed.'

Ross didn't say anything for a while, just fiddled with the remote as Shelly sipped at her drink, not sure now that her ally was gone how to deal with the sudden silence.

'You've got a lovely home.'

Shelly gave a small shrug, embarrassed at the sudden need for small-talk. 'It's not much.'

'It's great.' His eyes wandered around the room, taking in the jumble of photos filling every available space, the cushions scattered over the sofa, the toys dotted around the floor. 'It's a real home.'

Eyeing him over the top of her glass, Shelly realised then that he wasn't just filling an uncomfortable quiet patch, that his admiration was genuine, and for a reason Shelly couldn't even begin to fathom she felt the sting of tears in her eyes, something in Ross's voice reaching somewhere deep inside. 'So what happened at work this morning that was so awful?'

He didn't answer for a moment but when he did his voice was curiously hollow. 'They discharged Angus.'

Sitting up abruptly, Shelly tucked her long legs under her, shaking her head as she spoke. 'But I thought you went ahead and reported your suspicions...'

'Ah, but I'm just a lowly resident.'

'But surely...' Her voice trailed off as Ross shook his head.

'Dr Khan still insists that I've overreacted, that I'm a bit wet behind the ears, a touch too eager. He overrode my findings.'

'Ross, you're the most conscientious doctor I've ever met. As if you'd just jump right in if you didn't have valid reasons.'

'Not valid enough, obviously. Hell, Shelly, I've been in the outback for two years, I've seem more drama there than that lot can imagine.' He looked at her questioning face. 'I have,' he said insistently. 'I was the only doctor for two thousand kilometres and, believe me, I've had to make my share of decisions on my own two feet. I come back here and I'm treated like some sort of country bumpkin that's been starved of practising medicine, determined to create a drama when there isn't one. Well, I'm telling you that little kid is being abused—'

'Hey, Ross.' It was Shelly breaking in now, slightly taken back by the passion of his outburst but understanding where he was coming from all the same. 'I'm on your side here.'

'I know.' He ran a slightly shaking hand through his hair then forced that smile again. 'Let's watch the movie, shall we?'

But Shelly refused to buy it. Ross was hurting. There was something going on here that she couldn't put her finger on. 'Ross, why are you so upset about this?'

'A child's being abused, Shelly! Of course I'm upset.'

Mentally kicking herself, Shelly rephrased her question. 'I know it's awful, it eats me up too, but it's our job, Ross. Tragedies happen regularly in paediatrics. Any illness in a child is awful, but Angus seems to be really getting to you.' She watched as he shifted uncomfortably, as the shutters came down in those vivid blue eyes, effectively ending the conversation.

'You did everything you could, Ross,' Shelly pushed, not wanting to leave things there when he was so obviously upset. 'You've reported it, you've gone through all the right channels.'

'Fat lot of good that did.' Ross took a gulp of his wine as Shelly looked on thoughtfully. It was Ross not letting Shelly in now, and his obvious hurt not only upset her—it made her strangely uneasy. His disenchantment with the hospital unnerved her, made Shelly feel suddenly twitchy. How easy it would be for Ross to throw in the towel if things weren't going well at work, to head off back to his beloved outback, or wherever the mood took him.

'You can talk to me, Ross,' Shelly ventured. 'You've listened to my problems enough over the years. It goes both ways.'

'I'm fine.' Ross gave a shrug. 'Really.' As if sensing her sudden apprehension, he gave her a reassuring smile, stretching out on the sofa beside her, his winning smile back firmly in place. 'Let's just drop it, shall we? Talking shop is the last thing I need right now.'

She'd have been a fool to push it.

* * *

Even watching a slushy film that Shelly had seen maybe a hundred times felt special, sharing it with Ross.

It was so nice having someone to chat to, someone to grab a bag of chips from the pantry, someone to tell you what you'd missed when Mother Nature called and you couldn't wait for the commercials!

Topping up her glass as the movie ended, Shelly went to fill up Ross's but he shook his head. 'Better not. I'm driving.' He turned back to the television, not even a hint of innuendo hanging in the air, so why was Shelly blushing?

'Stay.' The single word was more of a croak really and as Ross turned his head Shelly shook hers. 'On the couch. I didn't mean…'

'But what would the neighbours say?' Ross laughed at the blush flaming over her cheeks. 'A strange man's car parked outside all night!'

'Well, they're going to have to get used to it over the next week and I'm sure they've got better things to worry about,' Shelly mumbled, filling up his glass. 'Anyway, it will be good for Matthew to see you here in the morning.'

A tourism commercial was playing now, inviting Australians to come and see for themselves the wild rugged beauty of the outback, and Shelly couldn't help but notice the way it held Ross's attention, one idle hand lifting his glass as he gazed at the screen.

'You really love it, don't you?' Shelly murmured.

'Oh, yes.' Putting his glass on the coffee-table, Ross stretched out on the floor. Propping himself up on one elbow, he fixed his blue gaze up at her. 'The time I spent in Tennagarrah was easily the best few years of my life.'

'Really?' Shelly shot him a slightly questioning look. Sure, the outback had its charms, but from the rap Ross was giving it, it sounded like he'd been living in paradise. 'But didn't you get lonely?'

'I didn't have five minutes to myself—there wasn't a chance to get lonely. It's like another world, Shelly. The entire community rallies round each other, respects each other. I can't even begin to describe the people, it's like one big family. You'd love it.'

'Oh, I don't think so.' Shelly shook her head firmly.

'You would,' Ross insisted. 'There's none of this arguing about policies, they're just so thrilled you're actually there. Without a doctor or midwife nearby, pregnant women have to leave their homes weeks before their due dates so they can be at one of the clinics when they go into labour. Can you imagine how hard it would be to up and leave your husband and children at the time you need them most, just to ensure a safe delivery?'

'It would be awful,' Shelly gasped.

'It happens there all the time, that's why they're so thrilled to have anyone medical there. You'd be treated like a queen, you being a midwife and everything.'

'I haven't practised for years.'

'You could do a refresher course,' Ross said easily, and Shelly found herself doing a double take. Ross was actually talking as if the idea had some merit! 'They're the most resilient people you'll ever meet, they have to be, which means nine times out of ten by the time they've called for medical attention, they really need it! You're using your brain, working on your own initiative every step of the way.'

'Well, if it's so good, why did you leave?' Shelly asked airily, while privately delighted that he had.

'There was a lot of talk about extending the centre I was at, making it into a small hospital.'

'So why would that put you off?'

'They wanted a three-to five-year commitment.'

Shelly almost laughed. 'And we know how much you hate the "C" word. Why's it so hard for you, Ross? Why, if you so clearly love the place, couldn't you commit to staying?' Her mind was only half on the question. Ross's T-shirt had worked its way out of his jeans, giving a teasing glimpse of a very flat, very brown stomach, blond hairs blazing a golden trail downwards, and Shelly had to force herself to concentrate, anticipating a vague answer about career progression or appalling wages, crippling social life, anything really.

Anything other than what came next.

'Haven't you worked that one out yet?'

Dark blue eyes were fixed firmly on her and Shelly took a desperate gulp of her drink, sucking in air as she realised her glass was empty, her eyes frantically seeking refuge from his direct stare. But no solace was forthcoming, just the decadent glimpse of his stomach, the muscular strength of his thighs and that very attractive bit in the middle that seemed to be working like a magnet to her green eyes.

'Worked what out?' Her voice was high, and she settled for the television. The late night news had started now, a touch of strange normality as her own world seemed to shift out of focus.

'Why I came back.' He'd knelt up now, tipping the last of the bottle into her glass as Shelly desperately feigned disinterest. 'I heard that a certain nurse I'd always had a soft spot for was suddenly single.'

When Shelly didn't respond he carried on regardless, his voice a velvet caress as it delivered his earth-shattering tale, as calm and detached as the newsreader talking easily about fires and bombs. 'More than a soft spot really. I never could quite get over her so when I heard her marriage was finished I figured I'd check things out for myself. Find out if things between us were as good as I remembered, see once and for all if the woman I'd been crazy about for so long was as gorgeous as I remembered.'

'And was she?'

The glass she was clinging to was being gently prised out of her hands, and she watched in stunned silence as Ross placed it very carefully on the table next to his.

'Better,' he whispered, his breath hot on her cheek, his lips moving in for a skilful kill, his lips when they brushed hers rekindling memories, the tiniest kiss they had long ago shared soldered into her subconscious; the rock, the strength he had provided wrapping around her again as Shelly closed her eyes, the soft warm flesh of his lips, the cool shiver of his tongue, the heady, all-embracing scent that filled her, the trembling reaction as his body pressed against her.

His kiss.

It was everything she'd secretly imagined.

And more.

Every electric brush of his hand, every tiny shared smile that had bonded them magnified now; culminating in this delicious lingering moment. Their lips moving, probing, as Shelly's fingers crept into the thick silken blond hair, the scratch of his jeans against her smooth long legs sending her stomach into freefall, the firm touch of his hands on her back as he pulled her closer.

And for a moment it felt so instinctively right it was easier to go with her feelings, to succumb to the moment, to die a little in his arms as his lips traced the hollows of her throat, as one hand worked its magic on the aching swell of her breast.

'Don't.'

The word was so at odds with how she was feeling, for a split second Shelly thought she was hearing things. But the sound of her voice was definitely familiar and it was her hands pushing him away, fiddling with her top, flicking back her hair, and it was her eyes frantically trying to avoid his.

'Why?'

It was a good question and one Shelly struggled to answer for a moment. Why shouldn't she just go on letting him kiss her, why shouldn't she just keep right on kissing him back? 'Because it isn't right.'

'It felt pretty right to me.' His hand was on her leg, fiddling with the hem of her skirt, with one tiny stray thread of lilac cotton. One tiny pull and the whole hem would unravel, one tiny touch and her resolve would weaken, and it was that thought that forced the words to come more harshly perhaps than intended.

'Is that what you're here for?' She looked at his nonplussed face. 'A week of regular sex?'

'What are you going on about, Shelly? I didn't plan for this.'

'Rubbish,' Shelly scoffed, erecting the barriers again, furious at herself for letting him near. 'But then again, you probably didn't. You're not one for master plans, are you? You're just happy to go with the flow, and why not? Let's see if poor old Shelly's fair game, it might make the next week a bit more pleasurable.'

'Let's get a couple of things straight here, Shelly.'

His hand moved, Ross moved, away from her, away from the sofa, and she felt the shiver of the air around her without him near.

'The doctors' mess mightn't be the most luxurious accommodation in the world...' His voice was very measured and deliberate, and Shelly realised Ross was the one in control here. Her heart was pounding in her ears, her mind reeling from the shock of the words she had delivered. She felt like a gauche teenager—one little kiss and already she was demanding explanations. She wanted the ground to open up and swallow her, but no such miracle was about to happen here. All she could do was fiddle with the thread on her hem that Ross had found as he delivered his stern lecture. 'But it suits me just fine. And to clear up another point before it jumps into your mind, neither am I here for your fabulous home cooking. Tuna casserole doesn't do it for me, unfortunately.'

Shelly opened her mouth to argue, to point out that she'd never intended to serve it to him, but she snapped it closed. Best to let him get his tantrum over and done with.

'And as for sex…'

Shelly deliberately tried to keep her face impassive, to think calm thoughts and stop that awful blush from darkening, not take a deep breath or raise her eyebrows or give him any indication that she was struggling with discussing that three-letter word with him.

'It's Saturday night, Shelly. I hate to sound arrogant, but if it's casual sex I want, I can think of several places where I'm more likely to get it…'

Her eyes jerked up for a brief second, not that she needed to see him. Long-limbed, impossibly tanned, that blond hair flopping over one navy eye, he could walk into any bar in Melbourne and half, if not all the women would subconsciously stand up and cheer.

Ross Bodey was one of those men.

One of those men that reminded women they were female.

One of those immaculate prototypes God threw out every now and then to show the world just how good he could make it.

And Shelly hadn't a hope in hell of holding him.

'I like you, Shelly.'

Still she didn't say anything.

'I've liked you for a very long time, you must have known that?' When she still didn't answer he carried on, but the stern assuredness had gone from his voice now. Instead, his voice was almost wary, questioning. 'There was always an attraction?'

'No.' Shelly shook her head. 'I was married.' The lie was audible and Shelly gave a tiny painful shrug. 'OK, I was attracted to you, Ross, like every other female in the hospital. Happy now?'

'I don't care about every female, Shelly. The only person's opinion I'm interested in is yours.

'Yours,' he emphasised. 'Maybe you're right. Maybe I did plan this, but later Shelly, much later. If we're going to have a relationship, it's hardly going to be able to proceed normally.'

Her vivid green eyes were frowning now. Ross talking about relationships was causing a massive mental overload and she had to forcibly drag her mind back to follow the words he was saying.

'We're not going to go to the movies, and have candlelit dinners and go to the theatre.' His grin was back now, almost. 'OK, maybe the movies, but with Matthew sitting in between us munching on popcorn while he watches a cartoon, well, it's hardly…'

'Romantic,' Shelly finished for him, but Ross just shook his head.

'Oh, it would be romantic, Shelly, but it's hardly get-to-know-you time. *This* is the get-to-know-you time. A fast-forward on the awkward dates, a chance to really get to know each other, to see if this attraction we both know we feel equates to the outside world.

'I shouldn't have kissed you then—you're right, it was too soon. I just never figured on this…' His fingers tapped his chest. 'Seeing you sitting there, so adorable, I just went with the flow, just followed my heart. Can you understand that?'

She did understand. His kiss hadn't been manufactured, some contrived move. As skilfully as it had been delivered, it had been loaded with instinctiveness, guided by her very own longing.

'We'll take things slowly,' Ross said tentatively as Shelly's face jerked up.

'You'll still stay?' Her voice was unsure. 'After all the things I said?'

'Shelly, what type of guy do you take me for? We had a minor disagreement, a few short words. Even if we'd had a full-scale row, do you really think I'd just up and go? Leave you and Matthew in the lurch?'

'No, of course not.'

He heard the uncertainty in her voice and knelt back down on the floor beside her, one hand resting on her chin, forcing those reluctant eyes to meet his. 'You don't sound very convinced.'

'I'm sorry,' She let out a long ragged sigh. 'It's me, not you.' She knew he was waiting for her to elaborate and after a moment, wrestling with her own demons, Shelly did her best to verbalise her confused emotions. 'Why would you stay, Ross? Why would you even want to be here? Matthew's own father—'

'Don't ever compare me to him.'

'I'm not,' she broke in quickly. 'You don't compare.' They didn't, Ross with his laid-back ways, his take-it-or-leave-it slant on the world, was a million miles away from the ordered, manufactured world Neil inhabited. A world where a little boy with special needs was just too damned hard, too not what they'd planned, too less than ideal.

Neil had his life planned.

Ross lived for the moment.

There was a question there in itself. Right there at the front of her mind. But gazing into the depths of his eyes, Shelly pushed it away. Pushed away the ordered, neat life she had made for herself and chose, perhaps for the first time ever, to go with the flow.

Sort of.

She couldn't just dive in here, there was too much at stake to throw caution to the wind and to hell with the consequences, but feeling his hand on her face, feeling the quiet strength of his body so very close, Shelly took a deep breath and dipped one very tentative, newly painted toenail into the water.

'I can't just tumble into bed with you.'

'I know.'

'We have to keep things under wraps, especially when Matthew's around.'

'Of course.'

'And I don't want anyone at work getting even a hint that there's romance in the air.'

Ross gave a slight grimace. 'Might have to do a quick renegotiation on that one. I'd say the whole ward knows that there's romance in the air.' He looked at her aghast face and grinned. 'There's sparks coming off the pair of us, Shelly, everyone knows.'

'Everyone except me,' Shelly mumbled.

'Rubbish.' Ross remonstrated good-naturedly, grinning ever wider until even Shelly managed a reluctant smile.

'I just wasn't expecting all of this.'

'All of what?' Ross asked innocently. 'From this moment on, I'm your official babysitter for the next week, nothing else.

'Nothing else,' he added, as Shelly shot him a very disbelieving look. 'You, young lady, can tell me when you're good and ready. My ego can't take being rebuffed twice in a row.'

He was joking, Shelly knew that deep down, but there was an element of truth to it all the same. Men like Ross Bodey wouldn't be turned down too often. Not that Ross seemed particularly bothered. He was picking his car keys up from the table.

'It's up to you, Shelly.'

'Where are you going?' Her heart sank a mile. All that chat about staying had obviously only been if sex had been on the agenda.

'To get my sleeping bag from the car.' He replied simply, not noticing the relieved look that washed over her as he wandered out to the garage, returning a couple of minutes later with the grubbiest offering of a sleeping bag Shelly had ever seen.

'I've got a spare duvet you can use,' she said quickly, wincing slightly as he unravelled the shabby swathe of material over her pale sofa. 'I can wash that for you in the morning.'

'You're not washing this,' Ross said in alarm. 'It would fall apart.'

'Exactly.' She would have pushed, would have nagged just a touch more, but Ross had pulled his T-shirt over his head and was now working on the buttons of his jeans. 'Is that it, then? Conversation over?'

'Yep,' Ross said easily. He was down to surprisingly white boxer shorts now and Shelly struggled to keep her eyes on his face, this blatant display of male sexuality not having the most soothing effect.

He watched her eyes dart down to his boxers and flick back quickly to his face, a furious blush working its way up her neck to her flaming cheeks.

'They accentuate my tan,' Ross said in a feigned effeminate voice.

'I never tan,' Shelly mumbled. 'I just go red and get a load more freckles.'

He was climbing into that disgusting bag now, looking up at her with innocent eyes, forcing an exaggerated yawn he stretched languorously. 'Turn the light off on your way out, would you?'

So that was it.

Not one goodnight kiss?

Not one further word of reassurance?

Not even one further attempt to discover the colour of her very new, very sexy knickers?

''Night, then.' Shelly flicked off the light and stood in the darkness for a moment.

''Night, Shelly.'

She turned, slowly. The bedroom was just across the hall and she walked the few steps rather slowly, her ears on elastic, hoping and simultaneously dreading that he'd call her.

Unzip that bag and pull her right on in.

Oh, she'd have gone.

In a second.

But Ross didn't call, even though she undressed slowly, even though she only turned the tap on to a dribble as she brushed her teeth, so that she didn't miss her summons, but the only sound that filled Shelly's ears was silence.

Slipping into bed almost frenzied with lust, she lay staring into the darkness, concentrating on keeping her breathing even.

All that talk, all that bravado about waiting, had dissolved in a flash the second he had undressed. The sudden low-key way Ross was acting was having the strangest effect.

Staring at the dark shape of the door, she almost willed it to open by mental telepathy, could almost see the outline of his spectacular body in the shadows. But just as she could take it no more, just as one hand was ready to throw back her duvet and call him to come to her, a rhythmic deep sound filled her ears, and Shelly shot back under the sheets like a scalded cat.

Ross was snoring.

Ross Divine-Body Bodey had had the gall to go and fall asleep.

CHAPTER SIX

SHELLY lay there for a moment when she awoke, trying to orientate herself, stretching in the warm bed then rolling back on her side and closing her eyes again. Since Matthew had been born, Shelly had never, not even once, just woken up.

Unless she counted the time she'd had her wisdom teeth taken out and Marlene had moved in for a couple of days, but that had been pain waking her, not the lazy, hazy feeling that came when one's body had actually had enough sleep. Normally little fingers were prodding her face or an alarm clock was buzzing in her ears. Stretching out, Shelly grappled for her alarm clock, her eyes widening in horror as she saw the hand edging past ten o'clock.

Her feet hardly met the carpet as she dashed out of the bedroom, her arms struggling to find the sleeves of the new dressing-gown she had bought in honour of her house guest, bracing herself for what she wasn't quite sure.

Chaos, as it turned out.

Ross's clothes still lay in a crumpled pile on the living-room floor, that awful sleeping bag half on, half off the couch, the curtains still drawn. Padding fast along the hall, she pushed the kitchen door open and the mess that greeted her made the living room look like a display from the Ideal Home Exhibition. Newspapers were everywhere!

Everywhere.

Cereal boxes and milk cartons littered the bench, bread, margarine, honey, Vegemite…

'Morning.' Turning from the bench like a phoenix rising from the ashes, she was privy to a glimpse of a very fetching smile, attached to a more than attractive body.

Ross had changed his boxer shorts, Shelly mentally registered as she took the steaming mug of coffee Ross was holding out for her. Still white, but littered with little red love hearts, and on anyone else they would have looked ridiculous.

'Why didn't you wake me?' Shelly asked, trying to ignore the chaos that used to be her kitchen.

'Because you're working tonight,' Ross replied with annoying simplicity as he guided her to the kitchen table. 'Do you want some toast?'

'Mummy sleep.' Matthew pointed a rather accusing finger in Shelly's general direction then broke into squeals of delighted laughter as she showered his sticky cheeks with a flurry of butterfly kisses. He was sitting at the kitchen table, his little pudgy hands working their way through the cartoon section of the newspaper and the endless reams of catalogues that came with the Sunday papers.

'Yes, Mummy did sleep,' Shelly muttered. 'Someone should have woken me.'

'Why?' Ross shrugged. 'We managed.'

Hot buttered toast was being placed in front of her, and without even bothering to ask Ross took it upon himself to slaver it in mountains of honey.

'Have you changed Matthew's nappy?' Half standing, Shelly sat back down as Ross rolled his eyes and gave an exaggerated sigh.

'Yes, I've changed it.'

'But how did you know where everything was kept?'

'You couldn't lose your keys in Matthew's bedroom.' He was talking with his mouth full, back to reading the papers and not bothering to look up. 'It's so neat I just looked under "N" for nappies. Couldn't quite work out where the talcum powder was kept, though.'

'He doesn't have powder, it's supposed to be bad for children's lungs or something.'

'Amazing we survived to adulthood, all things considered,' Ross said dryly, taking a slug of his coffee. 'We did all right, didn't we, Matty?'

She was about to correct him but stopped herself, not in time, though, for Ross to miss her intake of breath.

'Sorry, Matthew,' he amended.

They had done all right, Shelly conceded, nibbling on the edge of a piece of toast. She knew that she should have felt relieved that they were getting on so well and that Matthew had obviously taken to his babysitter. So why did she feel so edgy?

Because nothing was that easy.

Ross had swept back into their lives with effortless ease, had won over Matthew, installed himself in her home and even forced Shelly to admit to herself that she was hopelessly in lust with him.

There had to be a downside.

'OK, then.' Ross looked down at his watch. 'You can start cleaning now.'

'What are you talking about?' So deep in her daydream was she Shelly thought she must have missed something as she struggled to keep up with the conversation.

'Every day I'm going to stretch it out by another five minutes and by the time the week is up you'll be able to go half an hour without wiping down the benches.'

'You really think you've got me all worked out, don't you?' Shelly looked over the rim of her coffee-cup, a slightly mysterious smile playing on the edge of her full mouth.

'No,' Ross admitted. 'But I'm working on it.'

Shelly didn't clean the benches, didn't grab a garbage bag and start picking up the newspapers. For the first time in living memory, she ignored the mess and actually read the Sunday papers. The three sat in amicable silence, Matthew drawing erratic pictures over his pages, Shelly lingering over the colour supplements as Ross read all the newspapers from end to end, only rising every now and then to replenish their coffee-cups or open a packet of biscuits for Matthew.

And even though in the scheme of things it didn't add up to much, looking up from her magazine for a short moment, Shelly felt the swell of a lump in her throat, the tiny glimpse of domestic bliss such a cherished moment it would surely be etched in her mind for ever.

Her lazy day continued long into the evening. After some persuasion Ross took Matthew back with him to the doctors' mess to collect a few of his things and Shelly was privy to the decadence of an afternoon alone. Throwing together the quickest roast dinner a

Sunday had ever seen, Shelly bypassed the usual run under the shower, opting instead for a lazy soak in the bath before closing her eyes for a supposed ten-minute doze.

A bit more than ten minutes as it turned out.

A rather crispy roast was the order of the day, and by the time Shelly had bathed Matthew and put him to bed, Ross had made surprising inroads into the dishes.

'Why didn't you just load them into the dishwasher?'

'Because then I'd have had to embarrass myself telling you I'd no idea how to use it.'

Smiling, Shelly crossed the kitchen. 'It *is* a bit complicated actually.' Putting a tablet in the dispenser, she picked up his hand, leading his finger to the 'on' button.

'OK, Einstein, what are the rest of the buttons for, then?'

'Decoration.' Her hand was still on his and neither seemed in any particular rush to break the physical contact.

'Do you know what would be nice now?' Their hands had moved from the stainless-steel surface of the dishwasher and were now located rather more comfortably between them, Ross standing over her, his teasing grin matching hers.

'What?'

'Chocolate.' His eyes weren't on Shelly's, instead they were focussed on their mutually entwined fingers. 'A big slab of chocolate and a very sad movie.'

'Sounds wonderful.' That was an understatement. Curling up on the sofa with Ross would be the perfect end to a perfect day, and for once chocolate didn't even get a look-in.

'Ring in sick,' Ross grumbled as Shelly let out a gurgle of laughter.

'Which would entirely defeat the purpose of you being here.'

'I guess.' Puppy dog eyes were looking at her now and Shelly even amazed herself by imagining the wrath of Tania if she dared do it.

It would almost be worth it.

'I'd better get moving.' Reluctantly she retrieved her hand and padded off to her bedroom, pulling on her uniform and putting up her hair with indecent haste before applying only the briefest slick of lipstick. Shelly picked up her bag and hovered by the lounge door, watching as Ross, lying long and relaxed on the sofa, snapped in two the biggest bar of chocolate she had ever seen and for cruel effect pressed the remote control with gusto.

It would have been so easy to stay.

So frighteningly easy.

CHAPTER SEVEN

'How's the hired help?' Smirking slightly, Melissa sat down and dived into the box of chicken savouries Shelly had bought. 'Behaving himself?'

'Impeccably.' Shelly met her colleague's eyes, reddening as she crossed the line she had sworn Ross to and elaborated. 'Unfortunately.'

'I thought that was what you wanted,' Melissa was tucking into the savouries with gusto now, as Shelly concentrated on the feed she was giving.

'It is,' Shelly insisted, leaning back in the chair as the baby attacked the bottle. 'Or it was. I don't know, Melissa, I've set the boundaries, insisted he doesn't cross them, and now I'm annoyed that he's keeping to the deal that I set in the first place.' If she hadn't been holding a baby, so exasperated was Shelly she would have got up and paced the floor right then and there.

It was her fourth night on duty. Her fourth night of leaving Ross in her home and heading off to work. And no doubt in just a few short hours it would be the fourth time she would arrive home in the morning to two grinning faces and a house so untidy it was unrecognisable.

A house that felt completely like home.

'I was the one who insisted we didn't discuss things with anyone at work, and just look at me!'

'I'm not just anyone, though.'

Shelly let out the breath she'd inadvertently been holding. 'I know you're not. You must be just about sick of all my dramas by now.'

'On the contrary.' Melissa grinned. 'I love them, just so long as you keep on feeding me. When do your parents get back?'

'Sunday morning.'

'And you're off now until when?' Melissa asked with thinly disguised interest.

'I'm back at work on Saturday night.'

'So is Ross staying at yours for the next few nights, or going back to the doctors' mess in between babysitting shifts?'

Thankfully the baby started to fret and Shelly avoided answering for a moment as she placed the bottle on the workbench and leant the baby forward, massaging his back to bring up his wind.

'Shelly,' Melissa pushed. 'You can wind a baby and talk better than anyone I've ever known.'

'OK,' Shelly snapped, more annoyed with herself than Melissa. It was a question that had been plaguing her for the last couple of days and now as the clock crept toward four a.m. it was make-your-mind-up time. 'It would seem that the ball's in my court.'

'I've never held a tennis racket in my life.' Melissa grinned as she took another handful of savouries. 'You'll have to be more specific.'

'Ross has made it very clear the next move's up to me. If I ask him to stay the next few days…'

'He'll want sex?' Melissa asked eagerly, and Shelly shook her head and started to laugh.

'Melissa!' Shelly said indignantly. '*If* I ask him to stay it will mean I'm moving things forward, that I like spending time with him, that I want to spend more time with him.'

'Which you do,' Melissa said with annoying simplicity. 'And you can rub that back all you like but that baby's not going to burp for you again.'

'Look, what if I ask him to stay and by nine o'clock tonight I realise I've made a mistake? I can't just dash off to work...'

'You mean there'll be no safety net.'

'I suppose. What if I realise the mistake I'm making, what then?'

Melissa stood up and took the dozing baby out of Shelly's arms. Cuddling him in for a moment, she smiled down at the sleeping infant. 'You gave me a scare, little man, and just look at you now, all ready to go home tomorrow!' Her kind, shrewd eyes turned back to Shelly. 'Seems to me you're more worried what you'll do if you realise you *haven't* made a mistake.' As Shelly opened her mouth to protest, Melissa carried right on. 'That you, young lady, are more worried that waking up next to Ross might just be the best thing that's ever happened to you.' Shelly's mouth opened again but Melissa hadn't quite finished. 'What then, Shelly? That's what's really troubling you, isn't it?'

Waddling off, she left a troubled Shelly sitting at the desk and for something to do Shelly picked up the box of savouries, but a salty early morning snack wasn't going to solve her problems tonight. Even the slab of chocolate in her bag wouldn't bring answers.

Melissa, as usual, was spot on with her diagnosis.

What then?

Ross was five years younger than her and though their age difference would barely raise an eyebrow, those five years might just as well stretch to fifty.

Five years had seen Shelly marry, have a baby, divorce. Five years had led her to single motherhood, the only parent of a very special little boy, with all the joy that entailed on the upside but all the responsibility the permanent angst on the downside.

Whereas Ross…

Ross lived his life out of his backpack.

His five years had been spent studying, working, but most importantly living. Dancing, romancing, travelling, hot southern nights and all the promise a body like his would surely attract.

How could she hold him?

And if she did for a while, how could she possibly bear to lose him?

'You know Dr Khan?' Melissa was back. The baby had obviously settled easily and Shelly struggled to concentrate as the conversation turned back to work and the aging consultant that ruled the ward.

'We had an affair.'

Thank goodness she wasn't feeding a baby now! Shelly's jaw literally dropped open as her head swung around, positive she must have misheard!

'Thirty years ago, mind.' Melissa gave a shrug and took the box of snacks from Shelly's limp hand. 'I was in my twenties, a lot prettier and definitely a lot thinner.'

'Dr Khan!'

'Mushat. Mushi I used to call him.' She wasn't really talking to Shelly any more, her usual gruff voice was softer now. 'I knew from the start it wasn't going anywhere, we both did. Once his internship finished he was expected to go back to Pakistan and marry.' A thin, wry smile replaced the needs for words for a moment. 'Mushi wasn't going to rewrite the rulebook. He loved his family, loved his culture and more to the point he loved his wife-to-be. He had a wonderful marriage.'

'Did it carry on after…?' Shelly's voice trailed off as Melissa shook her head vehemently. 'He's a decent man, he'd never have cheated on his wife, it's simply not in his character. He loved her, Shelly, right up until she died last year. But for a while there he loved me, too.' Her eyes found Shelly's then. 'Like it or not, you've got a complicated life and men like Ross don't come by every day. Take your moments in the sun, Shelly, you don't know when then they're going to come around again.'

'Just because I'm a single mum with responsibilities, it doesn't mean I'm going to take any crumbs of comfort…'

'I'm not talking about Matthew.' Melissa ignored Shelly's snappish response. 'I'm talking about you. When Mushi and I broke up I cried like every other woman getting over a broken heart, and though I swore I'd never get over him, deep down I thought there'd be someone else, that one day what Mushi and I had would be just a warm distant memory.

'But that was it,' she rasped. 'That was it for me, Shelly. But as painful as it's been, I'm glad for the two years we had. For the two years I felt as beautiful and loved as every woman deserves to feel at least once in her lifetime.'

Pulling a couple of tissues from the workbench in front of her, Melissa blew her nose loudly and Shelly found herself doing the same.

'Is there any chance for you two?' Shelly ventured. 'Now his wife's…?'

Melissa shook her head sadly. 'There's too much water under the bridge now,' she said sadly. 'Since his wife died he's so brusque, and it's not just me that's noticed, even Ross was moaning about how much he's changed.

Sometimes when I talk to him about the patients, or the budget, or whatever the latest drama on the ward is, he's so far removed from the man I used to know I wonder if he even remembers how close we once were.'

'I'm sure he does,' Shelly said gently as Melissa blew her nose again and stood up. 'Perhaps you should try talking to him.' But her suggestion fell on deaf ears. Melissa looked up at the clock and started to pull out the drug trolley.

'And perhaps we should get on with our work.'

Work felt just like that for the rest of the morning.

Like work.

Melissa, embarrassed at revealing so much, turned into the ogre sister from hell and every baby in the place woke at six demanding to be fed, unmindful of the fact that Shelly needed to do some obs and write her nursing notes. In fact, by the time she turned the key in her front door any chance of preparing a speech for Ross was but a distant dream—not that it mattered.

Ross had obviously only awoken as her car had turned into the drive.

'Shelly,' he gasped as she came in and rather disdainfully eyed the lounge. 'I fell asleep. I was going to have it tidy for your last morning...'

'What, and spoil the surprise?' She started smiling as she watched him picking up blankets and toys. He was wearing navy boxers this morning, and if anything they made his tan look ever darker. 'Did the late night movie go on too long?'

'No.' He stopped his flurry of activity then and faced her. 'Matty got up a few times.'

'Matthew?' She wasn't correcting him. Shelly's forehead creased and for a second she felt the surge of panic familiar to mothers around the globe. 'Why?'

'I don't know if he had a dream or was just miserable.' Ross ran an exasperated hand through his hair. 'I checked him over but there was nothing wrong, I read him his gingerbread book, changed his nappy, gave him a drink, but he just wouldn't settle. I gave him some paracetamol just in case.'

'I'll go and check him, he's usually up now.'

'He's probably exhausted. Could he be teething?'

His question went unanswered as Shelly fled towards Matthew's bedroom.

'He's OK, Shelly, I checked him less than an hour ago,' Ross tried to reassure her, following her rapid footsteps, and though Shelly believed him, knew deep down what Ross was saying was true, until she saw Matthew for herself nothing was going to convince Shelly that her son was OK.

'Mum.'

She didn't even make it as far as the bedroom. A delightfully familiar bundle was running towards her smiling a very wide smile, little arms outstretched, dark hair sticking up at every angle—a tell-tale sign of the restless night he had spent.

'Hey.' For once Shelly ignored the fact she was still in her uniform and she scooped him into her arms, one hand instinctively sweeping his forehead, the nurse in Shelly checking for a fever as the mother in her rained kisses on his little pudgy cheeks. 'What's been the matter, little guy?'

'Mum,' Matthew said again, and it was all the answer Shelly was going to get, but all the answer she needed, and turning to Ross she gave him a relieved slightly embarrassed smile.

'I'm sorry you've had such an awful night. Normally he sleeps right through.'

'Don't worry about me.' Ross was standing right beside them, pushing his fingers into Matthew's fat tummy as the little boy giggled and rubbed his face in Shelly's neck pretending to be shy. 'And it wasn't awful. We had a bit of fun for while.' He gestured through the bedroom door to the biscuit wrappers and piles of toys on the floor. 'We had our own little party, didn't we, buddy?' His face turned to Shelly and he gave an apologetic shrug. 'I tried everything I could think of—read him that story he liked, I even sang to him. He wasn't upset or anything, he just didn't seem to want to sleep.' A large yawn ended Ross's sentence and he barely managed to lift his hand to cover it. 'I'd best head off to the shower.'

One final ruffle of Matthew's head and he turned to go.

'Woth.'

Turning slowly, suddenly Ross didn't look tired any more, an incredulous delighted look lighting his face as Shelly nearly danced on the spot in excitement, holding her breath as she waited for Matthew to say it again.

'Woth.' A little index finger jabbed in Ross's general direction and there was no mistaking the word that had spilled from his lips hadn't been an accident.

'Is that supposed to make up for keeping me awake all night?' Even though his voice was loud, Ross was grinning as he walked back towards them, the feigned anger in his voice not fooling Matthew for a second as he squealed in delight at the anticipation of another tickle, which was soon forthcoming. Shelly joined in the laughter, the strangest feeling bubbling in the pit of her stomach as Ross's face was suddenly serious, his voice low and soft. 'Well, guess what little man…? It does.'

Matthew's arms were pointing in Ross's direction now, and Shelly watched in wonder as the toddler slipped easily into his arms, resting his little head for a moment on the strong bare chest as Ross held him close for a moment, the expression on his face unreadable as Shelly stood silently watching this most precious moment. 'Best have that shower,' Ross said finally, reluctantly handing Matthew back. 'I'm sorry to leave you with all my chaos.'

'Don't worry about the mess. I'm just so grateful to you for helping me out, helping *us* out.'

'I haven't finished yet. We're still on for Saturday.'

Shelly nodded, wanting to speak, wanting to break in and tell him he didn't have to go, that he was more, so much more than just a babysitter, but the words simply wouldn't come.

'I'll come back after my shift and collect all my stuff.'

'You don't have to…' Her voice trailed off. The coming back she could certainly deal with, it was the thought of him leaving that hurt…

Ross was staring at her, his eyes willing her to continue, and for the longest time a loaded silence hung in the air.

'You'd better grab a shower. I'll rustle up some breakfast.'

It was such a paltry offer, such a pale offering compared to the words that were screaming from every taut nerve, but it was the best Shelly could come up with, and as Ross walked off she fought the urge to call him back, to somehow erase her last few words. To tell him she was feeling it too.

CHAPTER EIGHT

WITH Ross hogging the hot water, Shelly had to make do with a quick wash in the basin as Matthew danced around the *en suite*, squeezing her expensive moisturiser onto the tiles the second Shelly's back was turned.

'My one luxury in life,' Shelly admonished, picking up the empty tube and trying to scrape up the mess with toilet tissue. 'It will be all your fault if I dissolve into a mass of wrinkles and crow's feet now, and who's going to love me then?'

The innocent, bubbling smile that looked up swept away her vague annoyance.

'Ask a silly question.' Shelly smiled, placing Matthew on the bed as she slipped on some fresh undies and pulled on a skirt and top. 'And I'll love you too!'

Despite the fact Ross looked like a walking zombie—and a gorgeous one at that—Matthew didn't seem remotely tired after his night's exploits, tucking into his breakfast with gusto, then performing his usual disappearing routine as Shelly attempted to dress him, giggling away as she forced two kicking legs into a pair of shorts and two wriggling arms into a T-shirt. 'Now here comes the hard part,' Shelly muttered as Ross collapsed onto the sofa, only a skimpy fluorescent pink towel draped around his hips, his body glistening with the morning dew of his shower. Trying to tie the laces on Matthew's runners was a feat at the best of times, but trying to perform this task suddenly took on monumental proportions as Shelly saw Ross walk over.

He probably thought his assistance would make the task easier.

Flying solo to the moon without an oxygen tank would have been easier than attempting to tie Matthews's laces into two neat bows with six feet three of freshly showered tanned flesh hovering just millimetres away!

One damp, blond-haired arm brushed against her bare thigh as he expertly trapped one little fat leg and Shelly performed the amazing feat of tying a double bow, as opposed to brushing the shimmering drops of water of his forearm, as opposed to looking up and catching Ross's eye…

'I don't know how you do it.'

'Practice.' Shelly shrugged, planting a playful smack on Matthew's rapidly departing bottom as he scuttled away fully clothed.

They were still kneeling on the lounge floor and Ross rested back in his heels. 'Now I know why all the nurses head for the coffee-room as soon as they come on duty. I know that's where I'll be going.'

'Will you be all right—today at work, I mean?' She was genuinely concerned. Ross, for all his hectic social life, was a most conscientious doctor. Having listened with slightly envious curiosity to his party ways over the years, Shelly knew that despite the late nights and frequent dates and parties they were always held well away from a shift on duty.

'I'm wondering that myself. If I was heading off to a nice air-conditioned office and pushing a pen all day, I might try and bluff my way through.'

He gave a small shrug as Shelly chewed her bottom lip nervously. 'It's a bit different to examining children and writing up prescription charts.'

Ross nodded. 'Not much room for error there.

'Hey,' he added, seeing the guilt-tinged concern flood her face. 'I didn't come here for a holiday, I knew what I was letting myself in for. I'm not just exhausted from last night, I haven't really slept well since I've been here.'

'I thought you only got nightmares when you were on call.' It was meant as a small joke, a throw-away comment to fill the tiny space that was between them, but as she saw Ross shift uncomfortably, watched his cheeks darken, Shelly could have bitten her tongue off, realising with regret that she had embarrassed him. 'Ross, I'm sorry,' she said quickly as he stood up.

'Don't be.' Ross gave a brief smile. One hand holding his towel in place, he offered the other, which Shelly accepted, allowing him to pull her up from the floor. 'Anyway, it wasn't just nightmares keeping me awake.'

'I thought he'd been sleeping. You should have told me—'

'He has slept,' Ross interrupted. 'At least, apart from last night.' He sat back down on the sofa behind him and ran a hand through his damp blond spikes, his hair falling easily back into perfect place. 'I was just worried about him.' His blue eyes finally looked up from the floor he was staring at. 'It's different from being at work, isn't it? I just felt so, so…' His lips moved but no words came out and Shelly finished his sentence for him.

'Responsible?'

'That's the word. I kept thinking, What if his blankets have fallen off? What if he's called out and I haven't heard? What if—?'

'The laundry door isn't locked and he's wandered out?' Shelly grinned as Ross looked at her with a start.

'I checked it three times!'

'I do the same,' she admitted. 'Oh, I'm not so bad now, and Matthew wasn't old enough to wander when I first moved in here, but I can clearly remember those first few nights on my own with him after living with my parents. I never slept a wink.'

'So I'm not going crazy?' Ross gave a relieved laugh. 'When I gave him that paracetamol syrup I must have checked the dosage on the bottle about five times. How many times do I write up paracetamol syrup in a day's work? I guess it's different when you…' He didn't finish the sentence again and this time Shelly didn't jump in and help him, the unsaid word hanging in the air between them. 'I'd better ring Dr Khan and tell him I won't be in.'

'I'm so sorry, Ross.'

'Don't be. I've never had a sicky in my life, I'm too damn healthy. I reckon I deserve one. Can I?'

He gestured to the telephone, that simple polite gesture so completely unnecessary, but Shelly just nodded. 'Of course. I'd better get Matthew off to crèche.'

'Sure. I'll get my stuff together and be out of here by the time you get back.'

'You don't have to go, Ross.' The words tumbled out and Shelly could feel her breath bursting in her lungs as she carried on, speaking quickly. 'You can sleep here.'

'Are you sure?'

His casual question was loaded and Shelly gave a very quick nod. 'Of course.'

His eyes were on her and Shelly was eternally grateful to Matthew for choosing that moment to burst into the room. 'I'd better go.'

'He didn't sleep much last night.' Shelly hovered, as the bows she'd so carefully tied on Matthew's runners were undone and Lorna placed slippers on his feet. 'He might be getting a tooth or coming down with something. If he's miserable today—'

'We'll call you,' Lorna said firmly but kindly. 'Give Mummy a kiss, Matthew.'

His tears started then. Arching his back against Lorna, he held his arms out to Shelly, crying pitifully, calling to her as Shelly, her heart breaking, turned reluctantly to the exit door.

Even the fact she was exhausted and her bed was calling, even the fact Ross was waiting at home for her, wasn't enough to act as a barrier to the emotions that coursed through Shelly as she sat in the car park and battled the urge to simply run back in, to grab Matthew and just take him home.

Shelly, as usual, didn't even take her bag off as she came into her hallway and picked up the telephone, punching in the well-used number of the crèche.

'He's fine,' Lorna said patiently, though Shelly was positive she must be rolling her eyes as she spoke, wondering when this morning ritual would ever end. 'He settled as soon as you left.'

'Thanks, Lorna.'

'What happened?' Ross's concerned face came straight into view as Shelly put down the telephone.

'Nothing.' Shelly unravelled a very small piece of tissue she had bunched up in her hand and dabbed at her reddened eyes. 'Well, nothing unusual anyway. This is a regular event in this household.

'He hates crèche,' Shelly explained. 'And I hate sending him.' Her tears started again and Ross put an arm around her and pulled her in as she started to weep. 'He should be at home, Ross, with me. He's just a little boy.'

'You have to sleep, Shelly. You've been at work all night. Don't feel guilty for sending him.'

But she shook her head. 'I don't *have* to work. With the money it costs to send him to crèche, I'd almost be better off staying at home.'

'Then why don't you? I mean, if that's what you want to do.'

'Because it's a good crèche and he needs early intervention and stimulation.' Shelly gave a wry smile. 'I sound like the brochure. Look, I'm just tired and, like I said, this little drama happens every morning. You were just here to witness it, that's all. I'm fine really.'

'But are you?'

Shelly shrugged. 'Yes, I am. It's just hard sometimes, like we were talking about this morning. It's hard always being responsible, beating yourself up as to whether or not you're doing the right thing. It's just hard, dealing with it all on my own.'

'Then don't.'

Shelly looked up at him, startled. Her words hadn't been a cry for help, it hadn't been a leading statement, a secret invitation for Ross to help her, but it seemed that was the way he was taking it.

'Let me be there for you, Shelly.'

She shrugged him off, pushing him away. 'I wasn't telling you this in the hope—'

'I know you weren't,' Ross said quickly, one hand pulling her back and wrapping his arms firmly around her as she spoke.

'You don't know what you're saying.'

'Oh, yes, I do Shelly,' Ross said very clearly, but Shelly just shook her head.

'I'm going for a shower, and then I'm going to bed.' This time when she pulled away he didn't pull her back. ''Night, then,' Shelly said, even though it was nine a.m., even though sleeping alone today was the last thing in the world she wanted to be doing. Even though she knew she'd just broken his heart.

Ross just stood there as she left. Stood there with a helpless look on his face as Shelly dismissed him and headed for the bedroom.

Determined to face things on her own.

Five minutes alone was all that was needed. The first two took care of washing, one more to dwell on Melissa's words and two to realise that just metres away was all the man she had ever dreamed of.

A man who cared.

A man who clearly adored her.

Adored Matthew, too.

What on earth was she playing at?

Melissa was right.

If it couldn't or wouldn't work, then so be it, but denying herself the pleasure of Ross's touch, the bliss of being loved by him, even for a moment, for the fear of one day getting hurt was a poor argument, when saying no now would hurt more than Shelly could bear.

'Ross?'

He was sitting there just a step or two away from where she'd left him, the sleeping bag pulled out onto the couch, his shoulders hunched, his head buried in his hands.

'Ross,' she said again as he dragged his eyes up to meet hers. She stood shivering, wrapped in a towel, scared to move, terrified of where her next step would lead but knowing she had to, needed to, and so badly wanted to go there.

She didn't have to take it.

He crossed the room in a second. The message in her eyes displaying the clarity of her feelings, there was no need for words, no need for promises.

The promise was all there in his kiss.

Hot, sweet promises of the love and passion that was so much Ross, the strength the humour all there in the weight of his lips on hers as he held her close.

And how he held her!

Every last inch of skin pressing against her, the soapy musky scent of him dragging into her, filling her from the inside, her fingers coiling through his still damp hair, every touch a discovery of pleasure.

It wasn't just sexual desire that fuelled her, pushed her boldly on to impatiently tug at his boxers to glimpse the splendour of him, to take him in her hands—it was need. An unquenchable thirst for this most intimate knowledge, an irrepressible desire to know, to feel, to see all of him. To see him naked and splendid before her. She stared with aroused fascination, his body so perfect, so infinitely divine, and all hers for the taking. His arousal, an arousal *she* had instigated causing a fission of delight, a surge of feminine power, an overwhelming need to touch, to feel, to have him.

And Ross felt it, too.

There was nothing fumbling in his touch as he pushed away her towel, nothing blasé about the intake of breath as he stepped back a fraction, staring in undisguised admiration at her naked body, a tremulous hand reaching out. Slowly but with breathtaking stealth he moved his hand over the soft peach of her skin. Capturing her face in the palm of his hand, he slipped a finger between Shelly's softly parted lips, and in silent understanding she moistened the tip with her tongue, her breath catching in a strangled gasp in her throat as he teased one jutting nipple with his moistened finger, the pink swelling engorging with delicious pain, the other hand cupping the sweet welcoming warmth between her legs as Shelly groaned, her body arching toward his with an insatiable need to be filled, a voracious desire to be as close as man and woman could ever be.

He carried her to the bedroom, her bedroom, the one room he had been denied, the one area he hadn't inhabited.

Until now.

Now he filled the room as if it were his, laid her on the bed as if it were theirs, the dominant male in him surfacing gloriously as he climbed over her, nudging her legs apart with one powerful thigh, his lips scorching a blaze across her stomach, working their way across her swollen breasts and up ever upwards to her taut arched neck, finding her swollen mouth the second he entered her, her gasp of sweet, sweet pain filling his own mouth as he moved inside her, Shelly's most intimate vice gripping him ever tighter as they moved together, rose together, bucked together, the morning air filled with their gasps as their desires were met, their needs fulfilled. No question of prolonging the moment, their lust too overwhelming, the meeting of two bodies so longed for, so eagerly awaited, to have held back now would have been to deny the sweetest release of all. As he thrust ever deeper, Shelly's body spasmed beneath him, tightening, pulling, wrapping, pulsing, every inch of his gift such a pleasure to receive she gasped his name as her body shuddered beneath him, as he collapsed with exhausted pleasure on top of her, their glistening, warm bodies wrapped together in a mutual embrace.

'I've wanted this moment for so long, Shelly,' Ross murmured, kicking back the sheets and pulling her onto the pillows, covering her tenderly then wrapping his arms around her. 'I've dreamed of going to sleep with you beside me.' He was kissing her closing eyes now, his words so sweet that if they hadn't been so heartfelt they would have been corny, but she could hear the genuineness behind them, his touch so reverent, so wondrous, not for a second did she doubt that he meant every last one of them.

Waking in Ross's arms was almost as blissful as falling asleep in them. The hot afternoon sun blazed through a chink in the curtains, catching one of her long auburn curls that had strayed under his head, watching where the strawberry of her hair met the blond of his.

Melissa was wrong.

Strange, the thought that flicked into her mind.

Melissa was wrong, because one moment in the sun with Ross by her side simply wasn't enough.

If this was all there was, if the hurdles undoubtedly before them ultimately proved too great, if this was all there could be for them, though Shelly could never regret what had just transpired, though she would always remember it with love, the agony of losing him had suddenly magnified, and she shivered at the uncertainty that surrounded them.

Don't.

The word resounded in her ears as surely as if she'd spoken it, but Ross didn't stir beside her and Shelly wriggled onto her side, propping herself on her elbow and wallowing in the luxury of watching Ross sleep. Entrenching each and every feature on her mind, revelling in the beauty of awakening beside him, the gentle silence of the late afternoon, the inner peace she had finally found.

The solace she couldn't bear to lose.

A lazy eye peeped open, and he simultaneously smiled, not a hint of embarrassment, not a hint of regret between them, their bodies stretching languorously together, curious hands exploring each other.

'So this is what a sicky feels like. I think I might just have to ring Dr Khan and tell him I've had a relapse and can't come in again tomorrow.'

'There's still tonight,' Shelly said seductively. 'And still another hour or so before I have to pick up Matthew.' Her hand was tracing the muscular outline of his stomach now, edging downwards to the soft velvet warmth that reared eagerly to greet her.

'Time for some afternoon delight, then,' Ross mumbled into her hair as Shelly disappeared beneath the duvet. 'What are you laughing at?' Pulling her up level to his face, he smiled as she carried on giggling.

'I've been so wrong about you, Ross, so very, very wrong.' Another gurgle of laughter as she dived back beneath the covers. 'You are a natural blond after all!'

He just adored her.

Ross rose from the crumpled sheets while she showered to ensure a welcome cup of coffee met her as she stepped out of the *en suite*, rubbing her hair with a towel, then climbing back into bed to watch with blatant adoration as she dressed and brushed her hair.

'You're beautiful, Shelly.'

Up to that moment in time, Shelly would have blushed, would have laughed off his compliment, waved a dismissive hand, but this was no ordinary moment and this was no ordinary day. Under his loving gaze Shelly was able to accept the compliment with all the sincerity behind it. Putting down her brush, she turned from the mirror, a lump filling her throat as she took in the sight of him lying on her bed.

Her fantasy fulfilled.

'So are you, Ross.'

CHAPTER NINE

'HE'S been fine,' Lorna said cheerfully before Shelly even had a chance to ask. 'A little bit grizzly after his afternoon nap, but he perked up for music therapy. I think you might have a budding Spaniard here, you should see him shaking the maracas.'

The usual still damp 'painting' was handed to Shelly, along with Matthew's bag, and Shelly, loaded like a pack horse, staggered out to the car.

'Did you have a nice day?' Shelly asked as she strapped him into his seat. 'Lorna said you had fun making music.'

Little blue eyes stared back at her but Matthew didn't even attempt a nod. Driving home, Shelly kept up her usual light-hearted chatter, but for once Matthew didn't chat back happily from the rear seat.

Not that he ever actually said much, his vocabulary was too limited for any sort of in-depth conversation, but usually he babbled away, pointing to the cars, the clouds, anything that took his interest. Even when Shelly popped in a favourite CD and sang along to the music, checking in the rear-view mirror she found herself frowning when she saw that Matthew had fallen asleep.

He's tired, Shelly reasoned. After all, he *was* awake for most of the night.

'Hey, Matty!' Ross came out onto the driveway as Shelly pulled up. Opening the rear door of the car, he helped Shelly with the bags and painting as Shelly lifted her little sleepy-headed boy out of the car.

'He's worn out.'

'I don't blame him.'

Dinner was a quick affair, for Matthew at least, a bowl of his favourite fish fingers, and for once Shelly didn't push him with his vegetables when he firmly shook his head, rubbing his eyes and grizzling as he pushed away the bowl.

'How about an early bath and bed?' Shelly suggested, scooping him up.

'Do you want me to take a look at him?' Ross offered. 'My bag's in the car.'

'You've got a doctor's bag?' Shelly grinned.

'Yep,' Ross said with a just a hint of a blush.

'Did your proud parents buy it for you when you passed your finals?'

'I don't think they even noticed,' Ross said with an edge to his voice. 'I bought it myself.'

Shelly found herself frowning. That dark wistful note that occasionally appeared in Ross's voice was back, but just as she registered the fact, Matthew chose that moment to bring up his half-eaten dinner, crying as he retched, and any hopes of resuming the conversation flew out of the window as the next half-hour was spent bathing Matthew and mopping the floor, then visiting the shower for seemingly the umpteenth time that day.

'I'd hate to see your water bill.' Ross grinned as she came into the living room. He was holding a freshly bathed Matthew in his arms, reading him his bedtime story, and Shelly was grateful she could busy herself drying her hair, such was the lump in her throat.

OK, children were sick all the time, Shelly knew that better than anyone. But the night's mini-drama had been made so much easier with Ross there, and though he had examined him thoroughly, checked his ears and throat, gently palpated his stomach, it had nothing to do with the fact that Ross was a doctor and everything to do with him being a fabulous caring man. An extra pair of hands to help when Matthew was crying, to fetch the mop and make a couple of light-hearted jokes, someone to hold Matthew while Shelly dived in the shower, someone to reassure her that Matthew really was OK.

What a different scenario it would have been without him. Bathing a teary Matthew by herself, reassuring a fretful child alone, tucking him in, knowing she had to come out and face the mess she hadn't had a chance to clear up.

'Should I give him some paracetamol?' Shelly asked.

'He seems fine now.' Ross put his hand on his forehead. 'He's not hot.'

'Maybe he *is* teething,' Shelly said, coming over and sitting beside the snuggled-up duo and casting a worried eye over her son. 'Or maybe he's just overtired.'

'He might be brewing something, it might be better to keep him home tomorrow.'

'As if I need an excuse.' Shelly stood up and picked up her son. 'I'll just tuck him in.'

'Take your time.' Ross gently stroked the little head, a brief motion, a quick goodnight, but it was the *way* he did it, with such genuine tenderness in his voice, such genuine fondness in his touch that Shelly felt the familiar lump Ross seemed to generate fill her throat again. 'You'd better take this.' He handed her the rather dog-eared favourite book and Shelly padded off to settle Matthew, but for once even a little man made of gingerbread didn't raise a smile.

'What's up?' Ross noticed her frown as soon as she came into the lounge.

'Nothing,' Shelly said quickly, and then gave a sheepish smile. 'He just didn't want me to read to him. I shouldn't take it personally.'

Ross saw through her attempt at humour in a flash. 'Do you want me to take another look at him?'

Shelly shook her head. 'I'm just being neurotic, the poor kid's exhausted.' Forcing a smile, she turned for the kitchen and Ross followed her through.

'What are you doing?' he asked as he watched Shelly pull out various packets from the freezer.

'I was going to make something nice,' she said, trying to keep the weary note from her voice. 'Open a bottle of wine, you know, make tonight special. It's not every day someone like you comes along.'

'It's not every day your kid's sick,' Ross said perceptively. Pulling out a loaf of bread, he held it up. 'And as for making it special…' Her kitchen wasn't the biggest in Australia but it shrank even more as he crossed it in two short strides. Taking her in his arms, he held her for a moment. 'You've no idea how special this is to me. *I'll* make dinner,' he said, pushing her reluctantly away. 'You go and put your feet up.'

Toast and wine probably wasn't a connoisseur's delight, but sitting with Ross half watching the television as they chatted easily, for all the romance in the air they might just as well have been in a five-star restaurant with waiters lifting silver lids on flaming dishes and pouring wine the second their glasses met the tablecloth. And when Shelly started yawning, her four nights on duty finally catching up with her, Ross capped the romantic night off perfectly when she came back from checking Matthew and found him lying in her bed.

'How is he?'

'Sound asleep, he didn't even stir when I kissed him.'

He watched as she undressed, watched as she pulled back the duvet to slip into bed beside him.

'Go and put your nightie on.'

She shot him a quizzical look.

'Or your T-shirt or pyjamas, whatever it is you wear when Matthew's sick.'

His insight again floored her. 'You don't mind?'

Ross shook his head. 'He's the number-one guy in your life, Shelly, it isn't a competition. Go to him.'

'Thank you.' It seemed a strange thing to say, words that maybe didn't belong in the bedroom, but how many men, Shelly wondered as she tenderly kissed Ross goodnight and headed to her son's room, how many men at the very infancy of a relationship would give up a night of passion, would understand a mother's need, would be the one to instigate sleeping apart?

Only Ross Bodey.

At least he was the only one that sprang into Shelly's mind.

Slipping into the cramped single bed, Shelly pulled the warm body of her son near, kissing his soft cheek, pulling him into her. 'Goodnight, darling,' she whispered tenderly, laying her head back on the pillow. 'Mummy's here.'

'Ross!' Shelly could hear her scream echoing through the dark house.

It was her third attempt at calling him, the other two strangling in her throat and coming out as dry rasps as they did in a nightmare.

But, then again, this was a nightmare.

A living nightmare.

The bedroom door flung open and the room flooded with light as Ross flicked on the switch, and she watched the look of horror on his face as she turned her stricken one to him.

'He's having a fit!'

Instantly the horrified look faded, replaced in a flash by the calm, efficient doctor she had worked alongside as they'd cared for so many sick children.

Only this wasn't a patient, this was her son.

Shelly had already turned the rigid, jerking body of Matthew onto his side, but Ross crossed the room and took him from her, sitting beside her on the bed and placing the child across his knees, tipping his body downwards slightly.

'My bag's still in the living room.' His voice was calm but loud. 'Go and get it, Shelly.'

Through the darkened house she ran, obeying his order without question, but her mind was at odds. She should be on the telephone, calling an ambulance, summoning help.

She had help, Shelly registered briefly.

Ross was a doctor, he knew best.

Grabbing the bag, she stubbed her toe on the coffee-table as she dashed back but the pain that seared through her barely merited a thought. 'He'll be all right, he'll be all right.' The words were like a mantra, a steadying prayer, as she raced back to the bedroom.

'He's still fitting!' Her wail as she dropped the bag was verging on hysteria. 'He should have stopped by now, Ross, he should have stopped!'

Ross didn't respond to her cries. Matthew was on the floor now as Ross rummaged through the bag. He should be telling her it was over, that her little boy had stopped fitting. Instead, Matthew was still jerking, grunting noises coming from his distorted mouth, his eyes white as they rolled back into his head, and Shelly literally felt her knees buckle beneath her as she grabbed the chest of drawers for support.

'Go and call an ambulance, Shelly,' Ross ordered, his eyes never leaving Matthew as he undressed the rigid body. 'Tell them he's having a prolonged convulsion, that I'm giving him some rectal diazepam.

'Go!' he added, for the first time an anxious note making his voice waver.

Strange, the things you thought of when fear had got you by the heart. Shelly had picked up the telephone, thousands, probably hundreds of thousands of times, but as she picked it up this time she realised just why those three little emergency numbers were printed there.

The supposedly ingrained numbers seemed to have flown from her mind and Shelly had to physically read them to enable her to punch them in.

'Emergency. Which service do you require?'

How calm the voice sounded, how removed from the drama that was taking place in this very house. 'A-ambulance,' Shelly stammered. 'Urgently.' She wanted to hang up immediately to dash back to Matthew's side to see if he had finally stopped fitting, but instead she had to somehow recall her address, somehow tell them there was a doctor in attendance, the drug he was giving right now as she spoke, to somehow give them a clear picture of what was unfolding to enable an appropriate response.

'If you have an outside light, go and put it on now and open the front door. I'll stay on the line till the paramedics arrive.'

She didn't say thank you, didn't respond to the authoritative calm voice at all. Dropping the telephone, Shelly raced to the front door, fumbled with the lock and flicked on the light before racing back the length of the house, back to her son's side.

'He's stopped,' Ross said immediately, but there was no jubilation in his voice, and Shelly knew with a sinking heart why. The awful jerking had stopped but Matthew lay flat and lifeless. Just the rapid movement of his chest, the awful rattling noises coming from his mouth as he breathed showed he was alive. Lines she had never seen before were around Ross's eyes as he examined the floppy arms closely, tying a tourniquet snugly around one to bring up a vein. 'I need to get some IV access in case he starts again. Hold his arm for me in case he moves.' He made a tiny space for her alongside her son as he set to work.

Rows of tiny blood specimen bottles were already lined up in a dish. 'Tell me exactly what happened, Shelly.'

'He woke up a couple of times, he was just grizzling but he settled straight back to sleep.' She could hardly get the words out through her chattering teeth, and though she knew Matthew was past feeling pain, and she had seen the same procedure done so many times before, Shelly winced as Ross stuck the needle in Matthew's arm. Only this morning they had been holding him, but he had been kicking then, giggling and playing, not lifeless, not pale and flat with a horrible grey tinge to his lips…

'What happened then?' Ross dragged her back and Shelly took a deep breath, swallowing back the gulping tears that threatened to overwhelm her.

'Then *I* woke up. He felt hot. I was just getting out of bed to go and get the thermometer and check him when he vomited and then…then he started…' She began to cry in earnest, squeezing the little limp hand she was holding.

'Has he ever done this before?' Ross's voice was sharp. There was no time for sentiment, no time to comfort her. He was pulling back blood into the syringe now, then, replacing the cap on the IV bung, he started to squeeze blood into the various tubes.

'Never.'

'Apart from his Down's syndrome, has he any other medical problems?'

Shelly shook her head without elaborating.

'Any cardiac problems?'

'Nothing,' Shelly wailed. Down's syndrome children, apart from mental impairment and their recognisable features, often had other medical problems but till now Matthew had been blessed with good health.

'Is he up to date with all his immunisations?'

Shelly nodded, too choked up to speak, but as Ross pushed further she started shaking her head rapidly, hating the path Ross was taking.

'Has he had his meningitis vaccine?'

'He hasn't got meningitis.' The words stuck in her throat and she struggled to focus, watching with widening eyes as Ross attempted to push Matthew's head against his chest, checking for neck stiffness. 'He's had the immunisation, he hasn't got meningitis.' But Ross didn't seem to be listening to her. Instead, he was filling up a syringe with antibiotics as Shelly fought against the logic that seemed to be screaming at her, pleading internally for it not to be true.

Somewhere in the distance she could hear the wail of a siren, and she waited with bated breath for Matthew to rally, for the stomping of feet running through the house, for the flurry of activity that filled the small bedroom to somehow rouse her little boy. For him to open his little eyes and smile that endearing smile.

For Matthew to come back to her.

Instead, his beautiful tiny face was lost to her as a suction catheter and oxygen mask took their place, as red dots were placed on his chest and leads attached to a cardiac monitor, as bags of fluid were attached to the drip Ross had inserted. Shelly sank back on her heels, utter, overwhelming despair filling her as Matthew just lay there.

'Come on.' Ross's hand was pulling her up. Guiding her from the awful scene, leading her quickly into her bedroom.

'I don't want to leave him.'

'You're not leaving him,' Ross said firmly, pulling open her wardrobe. As if she were a child, he dressed her, guiding her shaking legs into shorts, pulling a T-shirt over her head, even putting her feet into her sandals, tutting gently when he saw the blood on her foot where she had stubbed her toe. 'Where are your keys?'

His question was so, so irrelevant the usually meticulous Shelly had to think, forcibly rake her mind to think where the hell they might be. 'In my bag.'

'This one?' Ross held it up and as Shelly nodded vaguely, the gut-wrenching nausea that had been ever present since Matthew had started fitting overwhelming her now.

'Ross, I'm going to be sick.'

He didn't even bat an eyelid, just guided her to the *en suite*, running a towel under the tap to wash her face down afterwards, which he passed to her as easily as if he were passing her a tissue. 'Come on.'

The night air was warm as she stepped outside. They were loading Matthew into the ambulance now and Shelly vaguely registered the concerned neighbours standing and watching on the nature strips, dressed in shorts and nighties, brought out by the flashing blue lights of the ambulance and police car that was parked beside it. But she had eyes only for the stretcher and the tiny, precious bundle it carried.

'Just wait here, love.' A policewoman held her arm and gestured for Ross to go inside the ambulance.

'I'm his mother,' Shelly argued, but it was pointless. 'Why are the police here?' she asked, bemused.

'We're going to provide an escort.'

The policewoman's hand was on her shoulder, a quiet gesture of comfort and support, but Shelly was way beyond comforting. Every crackle on the radio, every garbled message making her jump with alarm as she waited, waited to be allowed in to her son.

'What's taking so long?' Shrugging off the hand, Shelly lurched forward as Ross stepped down from the ambulance, his face grim, the blue light flashing, his skin unusually pale, and he took her hand as he spoke.

'He had another fit,' Ross started gently, 'just as they got him inside. We stopped the fitting but…' He was swallowing, trying so hard to look at her, trying so hard to be the strong one. 'He stopped breathing for a moment.' His hands tightened around hers as she gave a strangled sob. 'We've intubated him, he's heavily sedated.'

If he hadn't been holding her she was sure she would have sunk to the ground, but there was no time for dramatics. She needed so badly to see Matthew, however bad he was, and Ross seemed to understand that, gently helping her up into the ambulance, the paramedics nodding briefly as they moved some equipment to give Shelly some room to sit down.

'We've got a police escort,' the paramedic said kindly. 'We're going to have him at the hospital in no time. You just sit there and we'll work on.'

His instruction, however gently said, was clear.

There was nothing now Shelly could do.

The ambulance screeched off, hurtling through the darkened streets, its lights flashing, siren occasionally wailing as they braked near traffic lights then accelerated when the road was clear, playing a strange game of chase and catch with the sleek lines of the police car. And Shelly sat there, her teeth chattering, her body sliding along the seat with the motion of the ambulance, her white-knuckled hands holding the seat beneath, her red eyes staring, pleading at the inert body of her son as Ross and the paramedic worked on, squeezing the oxygen into his little lungs, the steady drip of the infusion, the loud rapid blips emanating from the cardiac monitor, so, so fast for a little boy so very still.

The familiar sight of her hospital only terrified Shelly more. Here the awful dream became a reality as she watched well-known colleagues huddling into their theatre greens suddenly move as the ambulance approached, wrenching open the rear doors before the vehicle had even come to a halt, racing to get Matthew inside, to the life-saving equipment and trained expertise he so desperately needed.

Someone, Shelly didn't even notice who, led her inside, showed her into a small neat room where she was left, trembling, hugging her arms around her, waiting for some news, waiting for someone—anyone—to come and tell her just what the hell was going on.

'Hello, Shelly.' A vaguely familiar face appeared at the door and Shelly frowned as she tried to place it. 'I'm Dianne, the receptionist. I just need to get a few details from you.'

'Have you heard anything?'

Dianne shook her head. 'One of the nurses or doctors will be in to see you just as soon as they can.'

Shelly stumbled through the form, giving Matthew's name, his age, his date of birth, his address.

'Does his father live at the same address?' Dianne asked in the same tactful voice Shelly herself had used so many times before.

'No.' Shelly hesitated. 'We're divorced.' She waited for a ream of other questions but they didn't come for now. Dianne clicked off her pen and slipped it back into her pocket.

'I'm a nurse,' Shelly said in last futile attempt to gain access. 'I'm a paediatric trained nurse, I work here! I should be with my son.'

'You're a mum tonight,' Dianne said gently, the compassion in her voice steadying Shelly for a moment. 'Let them do their work.' Gently she guided her to a chair and handed her a box of tissues. 'Is there anyone you want to call, anyone I can ring for you?'

Shelly shook her head. 'I'd rather wait till I hear some news.'

'Hopefully it won't be too long.' Dianne gave her arm a small pat. 'I'll put my head in as I go past, remind them you're in here.'

'Thank you.'

Till then Dianne had always just been a receptionist, a woman Shelly nodded to sometimes in the car park or someone she grumbled to occasionally when the labels from Emergency were missing from the files, but tonight Shelly realised there was so much more to her job, that the administrative personnel who worked in a hospital were just as valuable as the nurses and doctors, and the patients that came through the door affected them just as much as the frontline staff.

'How is he?' Shelly jumped up the second Ross finally entered, but he gently pushed her back down into the chair.

'The same, Shelly, they're still working on him.'

'Is he fitting?'

Mercifully Ross shook his head, but the elation was soon doused. 'He's very sick, Shelly. Dr Khan's in with him, and he thinks that it *is* meningitis.'

'But I had him vaccinated.'

'Shelly, you know as well as I do that the vaccination only protects against one strain of the disease. Dr Khan seems to think it's bacterial, but we won't know anything for sure until the test results start coming in.'

'Can I go in yet?'

Ross shook his head. 'It's better you stay here, Shelly.'

'What about you? Why aren't you in there with him, doing something?' Her voice was starting to rise again, angry, scared eyes turning on him.

'They told me to wait outside. I was getting upset…' His voice trailed off but Shelly didn't say anything to fill the silence, just sat starting vacantly ahead, waiting, willing, praying for some news.

How many cups of tea went cold Shelly lost count, but the first rays of morning light were filtering through the curtains when the distinguished but weary face of Dr Khan finally sat in front of them. He nodded briefly to Ross before turning his full attention to Shelly.

'Matthew is a very sick little boy.' His words were measured, delivered slowly but surely, and he sat quietly for a moment to let them sink in. 'We're going to move him up to Intensive Care shortly. At the moment we've got him sedated and on a ventilator.'

'Is it meningitis?'

Dr Khan nodded. 'All the signs at this stage point to bacterial meningitis. Now, I understand from Dr Bodey that Matthew, apart from his Down's syndrome, is a well child, that he's got no other relevant medical history.'

'He's fine.' Ross's arm was around her and Shelly allowed herself to sink into him for a moment. 'Or at least he was. He's been a bit grizzly. I should have known, I should have bought him up sooner, should have—'

Dr Khan held up his hand. 'This is no one's fault. No one's,' he reiterated. 'Meningitis can strike very quickly. The early symptoms are vague and mild. No one could have predicted this.'

Shelly felt Ross's arms stiffen around her, and as she sat up slightly she looked at the utter despair on his face, the pain embedded in his eyes, and she knew she should somehow comfort him, say she understood what Dr Khan was telling her, that this horrible situation wasn't his fault. But she was too emotionally raw, too scared, too drained to worry about Ross's feelings at that moment. All she wanted was to see Matthew.

'Can I go to him?'

'I'll ask one of the nurses to come and fetch you.' He stood up and briefly looked down at his notes. 'Shelly…' She heard him clear his throat, felt his discomfort. 'As I said before, Matthew is very sick indeed. We're doing everything we can for him…'

'How long will it be?' Shelly's eyes looked up, pleading for a shred of comfort. 'How long until he stabilises?'

There was the longest pause, for an age the horrible sound of silence filled the room and Shelly willed Dr Khan to speak, to inject some measure of hope, some time-frame to cling to.

'We're taking things minute by minute at the moment. I know that you aren't with Matthew's father, but I think you should inform him that Matthew is here.'

'He doesn't see him,' Shelly said quickly. 'He just pays half the crèche fees and gives the odd present here and there…'

Dr Khan's eyes were back on his notes and Shelly felt her heart sink, the realisation of the direness of the situation magnifying as he spoke.

'He needs to know how sick his son is, Shelly. He needs to be given an opportunity to see him…'

Dr Khan didn't say anything else, his unfinished sentence hanging in the air as he slipped out of the small room, leaving a shell-shocked Shelly sitting there trying to absorb the hell behind his words. As Ross's hand found hers she instinctively tightened her fingers around it, clinging on for dear life to the one comfort in this whole bleak wilderness, her eyes turning to him filled with despair. 'Is he telling me Neil should be here…?' Her words caught in her throat and struggled to speak, to articulate the hardest words of her life, mentally willing Ross to soothe her with a smile, to tell her she was overreacting. But instead he pulled her close, buried his face in her hair and wept alongside her as Shelly carried on talking. 'That I should give him the opportunity to say goodbye?'

CHAPTER TEN

'I WISH it was you looking after him.' Shelly gave a weary smile to Melissa as she sat on the empty seat beside her. 'They've told me to wait in here while they do some chest physio and take some X-rays, that's as much as I've been told. I don't know if it's because I'm a nurse they assume I know all the answers, or that they're worried they'll upset me.'

'Maybe they're just busy looking after him,' Melissa suggested gently, picking up the half-drunk cup of chocolate from the table and handing it to Shelly. 'And I *will* be looking after him soon. Once he gets out of Intensive Care he'll come to the children's ward.'

'If he comes out.' Shelly's voice was flat. The tears had stopped hours ago and she was operating on autopilot, her mind almost detached from the true horror of it all in some strange attempt at self-preservation.

'He *is* going to come out.' Melissa's voice was confident, determined. 'He's going to pull through, Shelly, you have to have faith.

'Where's Ross?' Melissa asked when Shelly didn't respond, just stood up and moved to the glass window, her eyes staring helplessly to where her son lay, surrounded by doctors, nurses, tubes, machinery.

'He's gone to find the contact numbers for my parents. I was going to let them finish their holiday, they've only got another day...'

Her dry eyes suddenly welled, the gripping fear she was so desperately trying to control suddenly gushing in from all sides with such force Shelly thought she might be knocked to the floor. Melissa rushed over, wrapping her arms around her friend, trying to somehow comfort her, despite knowing there was no comfort to be found.

'Shelly.'

The familiarity of the voice calling her gave Shelly no comfort. Looking up, her whole body seemed to tense as she saw Neil standing in the doorway of the intensive care waiting room, clean-shaven, dark-suited, his shirt crisp and white, a plain navy tie luxurious in its simplicity.

Strange, the things one thought.

Strange, how the tiniest, most insignificant detail could take on humungous proportions.

'You look like you're on your way to work.'

He didn't respond to her statement. Instead, he walked over to the window, nodding briefly to Melissa.

'How are you, Neil?' It wasn't the friendliest of greetings but, then, Melissa had been the one pulling the tissues out of the box for the last couple of years, comforting her friend and colleague through the minefield of divorce, the roller-coaster ride of bringing up a special needs child. She gave Shelly's shoulders a squeeze. 'I'd better get back to the ward. I'll come back up in my coffee-break.'

'So how is he?' Neil was looking through the glass now and Shelly watched with something bordering on compassion as she watched him start as he saw Matthew lying there.

'The same as when I called. Apparently no news is good news for a while. Until the antibiotics take effect we just have to wait and see.'

'But they'll work?'

Shelly gave a brief but painful shrug. 'There are no guarantees.'

They stood in mutual silence, staring through the window, watching as the radiographer pushed the machine forward to take a chest X-ray. A nurse, looking up, gave an apologetic smile then pulled the curtain on them, blocking their view, assuming perhaps it was less painful that way.

'You'll be able to see him soon.' Vaguely, Shelly registered Neil's discomfort, a slight shift as he moved his feet, taking breath in as if he was about to speak, but she was too wrapped up in Matthew to tread gently. 'What, don't you want to see him?' she asked incredulously.

'It's not that I don't want to,' Neil responded quickly, running an uncomfortable hand across his face. 'Cecile just wanted me to check that it would be OK.' He at least had the grace to blush as he continued, to attempt an apologetic shrug. 'She's pregnant, Shelly.

Only just, you know how dangerous things can be during the first trimester.'

'The first trimester!' Shelly gave him a wide-eyed look, the biting sarcasm clear in her voice. 'My, we are taking an interest!'

'Shelly don't,' Neil shook his head. 'You can't blame Cecile for being concerned. Hell, I'm concerned. I don't think I could go through it all again if something went wrong this time.'

His lack of sensitivity shocked even Shelly, who had truly thought Neil was beyond hurting her any more. 'If I remember rightly,' Shelly said, her voice wavering with emotion, 'you didn't go through it the first time.'

'I didn't come here to fight.' He was looking through the glass. The curtain was being pulled back, the nurse gesturing they needed a couple more minutes. Shelly watched as he stared at his son, an expression she couldn't read on his face. 'I'm sorry, Shelly, I didn't mean for it to be like this for the three of us.'

'Do you think this is how I'd planned it?'

'I just couldn't cope when I found out he was handicapped. I thought that maybe once he was born I'd come round, but I didn't, the whole thing terrified me. I couldn't just accept it the way that you did.' He was nearly crying now, but Shelly felt no sympathy. 'You're a better person than me.'

'I'm his mother,' Shelly said in a cool voice that defied the emotions coursing through her. 'My love for him isn't negotiable.'

'You're stronger than me...'

'Don't make excuses, Neil.' There was a bitter note creeping into Shelly's voice, coupled with an emerging resilience. 'You wanted the perfect job, the perfect home, the perfect family.' Her green eyes turned to meet his. 'And I hope you get it with Cecile, I hope for her sake that she and the baby can live up to your expectations.' She looked through the window at Matthew, so small and so innocent, struggling so hard just to stay alive. 'All that little boy wants to do is love, that's it. It's as simple and as beautiful as that.'

'Don't make me the bad guy here,' Neil was crying now, taking out a perfectly ironed handkerchief and blowing his nose loudly. 'I know I'm not perfect. I just couldn't cope. Not everyone's like you, Shelly, not everyone's perfect!'

But Shelly refused to accept his excuses, her tired eyes turning to him. 'He's going to get through this, Neil, and when he does, you can forget about the crèche and the occasional present, you can forget about reluctant access visits. Matthew deserves better. You're in or out of his life, not somewhere in between. His attention span's too short for someone to just drift in and out. He needs constancy, he needs a secure world, and I won't let you hurt him.'

She was letting him off the hook, offering him an out, a chance to get on with his life, and the disappointment, the pain she felt when he nodded was all for Matthew.

'Can I sit with him?'

Shelly nodded as a nurse gestured for them to come around. 'Do you want some time alone with him?'

'Thanks.'

Shelly watched through the window, watched with a heart that felt it wasn't beating any more as Matthew's own father hovered tentatively by the bedside, an awkward hand patting his son's, a helpless look on his face as he eyed the equipment, blowing his nose and wiping away tears.

She certainly wasn't perfect, Shelly thought ruefully. Perfect people were able to find forgiveness, and as she watched Neil pick up his briefcase and turn away there was certainly no forgiveness in her heart. She couldn't even muster up the emotion to hate him. Instead, she made her way out of the waiting room, sat by Matthew's bedside and laid her cheek on her little son's hand.

No one would ever hurt him again.

'Why don't you try and rest for a couple of hours?' Julie, the ICU sister, offered gently. 'Melissa said you've just finished a stint on nights, and you obviously didn't get any sleep last night. You must be exhausted.'

'I'm fine,' Shelly lied, her ashen face not even looking up at the kind voice. 'I really don't want to leave him.'

'I know.' Julie was perched on a high stool at the end of the bed, massive sheets of observation charts on the workbench in front of her, monitoring every tiny variance in Matthew, his observations, the drugs he was receiving, his fluid input and output, rows of red and blue lines all charting his progress. 'But you need to sleep.'

Shelly liked her. Liked the calm way she responded to the alarms that seemed to go off with alarming regularity, liked the way she spoke to Matthew as she nursed him, the way she let Shelly help wash him and comb his hair and do his mouth care. Julie was very young and very pretty, but the depth of her knowledge belied her youthful face and slowly Shelly was starting to trust her.

Shelly had even accepted that the lack of information coming from Julie wasn't an attempt to keep her in the dark. No one knew the outcome.

'There's a relatives' room just along the corridor. I'll send someone for you the second there's a change, and if he stays the same I'll come and get you myself when I go to lunch. Shelly, you know you're going to be useless for Matthew if you make yourself ill.

Hopefully in a few days he'll be running you ragged, demanding drinks and sweets.'

The line Julie was using was so familiar, one Shelly had used herself so many times before, and the exhaustion, emotional and physical, was starting to catch up. Every bell, every alarm seemed to be grating in her brain, everything making her jump, Neil's departure playing over and over in her mind like some ghastly video she couldn't turn off.

'Julie's right.' Ross was back, looking refreshed in comparison to the pale shadow of Shelly. He was wearing shorts and a T-shirt, his tan so ridiculously healthy-looking it made Shelly feel like a corpse in comparison. 'You have to sleep.'

'Hi, Ross.' Julie pulled her charts into line, moved over just an inch to let him see them. Try as she may, Shelly couldn't fail to notice a certain warmth in Julie's voice, a certain perkiness appearing, her pleasure in seeing Ross blatantly evident. 'Did you want to take a look at Matthew?'

Ross shook his head. 'Sorry, Julie, I didn't explain myself, did I? I'm actually here with Shelly and Matthew. I'm off duty today.'

'Oh.' Shelly saw the flicker of confusion on Julie's pretty face, her eyes dart questioningly to Shelly, the tiniest, almost insignificant gesture but with the hugest ramifications.

The impossibility of this couple so evident in her eyes.

Julie hadn't been flirting, at least, no more anyway than every other female in the building when Ross was about. After all, even the most happily married woman sucked in their stomachs in honour of Ross, he was that type of guy. The world brightened a touch when Ross was around, Shelly knew that better than anyone.

'Come on.' Ross pulled Shelly up from the chair where she sat and she hovered for a moment. 'What about you?' she argued, reluctant to leave. 'You've been up, too.'

'I'll have a rest later. Go on. I'll sit with him.'

'How did you go with the travel agent?'

'All taken care of. They're going to tell the rep and check the flight availability before they tell your parents.'

'Thanks for that.'

'Here.' He handed Shelly her own overnight bag. 'I'm not too sure if I've packed all the right things but I gave it a go. Go on,' Ross said gently, 'go and lie down.'

She watched him tenderly stroke Matthew's hair, and it was so, so different from Neil's formal, uncomfortable gestures, so far removed from the wooden emotions of Matthew's own father. But Ross wasn't Matthew's father, Ross didn't need to be here…

'When's Neil coming?'

'He's been…' She watched a frown mar his face, his mouth open to speak, and she carried on regardless. 'And gone already.'

For a second she didn't say anything, just stared at the two people she loved most in the world, the two people who mattered.

Two worlds so far removed.

'Ross, can I speak to you a moment?'

'Sure.'

Back to the waiting room Shelly went, back to the coffee-machine, the magazines, the brown corduroy cushions with the button in the middle missing. She knew every inch of the room, every peeling piece of paint, and Ross stood there in the middle of it, his face full of concern as he waited for her to speak.

'This isn't going to work.'

'What isn't?' He sounded genuinely bemused, as if he had no idea in the world what Shelly was about to say.

And maybe he didn't, Shelly reasoned. Perhaps he hadn't given any real thought to what it was all about. He had just drifted into her life without question, just assumed it would work.

'Us.' She let the single word sink in before she continued. 'Like I said, Neil's just been and I've told him I don't want him in our lives. I don't want people drifting in and out. I want Matthew to have security…'

'I can give him that,' Ross argued, coming over, but Shelly put her hand up.

'You can't, Ross.' Tears were coursing down her cheeks and she didn't even bother to wipe them. 'You're twenty-seven years old, you could have any woman you want, and one day you're going to look at me and Matthew and all the problems—'

'Don't even go there,' Ross interrupted furiously. 'Do you think I'm that weak, that some pretty little thing would just have to bat her eyes and I'd be off? Shelly, I adore you, I'd never betray you.'

He sounded so utterly convinced, so sure of his feelings, Shelly almost believed him, but it wasn't just Ross's drop-dead gorgeous looks on the agenda and Shelly reminded herself of that as she stood her ground. 'How long is your contract here, Ross—three months, six?

'How long, Ross?' Shelly pushed when Ross didn't answer straight away.

'Three months.'

'And what then, Ross? The outback again, Asia or Africa perhaps? One day you'll move on. You might not think it now, but one day you'll look around you and realise just what you've taken on and I can't blame you for that, can't blame you for feeling the way any person would, but I can't put myself through it, can't set Matthew and me up for another fall. I don't think we'd survive.'

'Shelly, look at me,' Ross urged. 'Look at me and for once in your life listen! I don't know where I'm going when this contract ends, that all depends on you. I came back *because* of you, I didn't just drift in. You're tired, you're upset...'

It would have been so easy to give in, to accept his words, but Shelly knew she had to be strong. However unwitting, she'd seen the incredulous look in Julie's eyes, seen the improbable couple they made, and however much Ross couldn't see the bitter end they surely faced, Shelly could.

'You're not what Matthew needs.' She watched his face slip. His eyes seemed to literally sink, his shoulders lowering as he exhaled slowly. All the fight of before seemed to leave him then, the struggle to make her listen, to see his point disappearing as if a light had been switched off. 'Matthew deserves stability, and I'm going to make sure he gets it. You can't provide that, Ross, no matter how much you might want to. What I feel doesn't come into this, Ross, it can't. What I'm trying to say is—'

It was Ross who held his hand up to silence her now, Ross who shook his head. 'Don't, Shelly, I think you've made yourself perfectly clear.' His face had a weary dignity about it. 'You have to do what's right by Matthew and, like it or not, I have to respect it. Hey, who am I to argue with a statement like the one you've just made?' He made to go but at the door he paused, turning for a second, and Shelly had to force herself not to rush over to him, his pain so evident she felt it, too. 'Maybe you're right, Shelly, maybe I'm not cut out to be a parent.' His eyes met hers then. 'But I'd have given it my best shot.'

CHAPTER ELEVEN

IT WAS the loneliest twenty-four hours of Shelly's life.

Surrounded by friends and colleagues, her parents ringing on the hour every hour as they awaited their flight home, endless trips to the waiting room to update anxious visitors on Matthew's progress, friends who had made the trip despite knowing they wouldn't be allowed to see him. Even Lorna from the crèche came, openly crying when she looked through the glass, wondering as everyone did if she'd somehow missed something, if there was something she could have should have done differently. But despite all the activity, all the concern all the love and concern that surrounded her, Shelly felt isolated. As if she were inhabiting an alien planet, even normal conversations, basic exchanges seemed to be taking place in another language.

The only light moment to an otherwise awful day was when she finally, at Julie's insistence, left the ward for the briefest of showers. Ross, love him, had indeed packed and as she looked at the handful of underwear tossed inside she paled at the thought of him rummaging through her knickers drawer, making a mental note to toss out every sensible pair of undies she possessed the second she got home.

She longed for Ross's easygoing nature, for his insight, for his different perspective. Longed for him to rub her weary shoulders the way only Ross could, to inject his easy optimism into this most awful situation and, Shelly admitted almost guiltily, she longed to lie down on the bed Julie kept suggesting she try, and leave Matthew in Ross's tender loving care.

But it was way too late for that.

There had been such hurt in his eyes, a hurt beyond what Shelly had ever imagined there might be, a depth to his pain she hadn't anticipated.

Neil had been relieved.

Ross had been devastated.

* * *

'Darling.' Marlene looked so tanned and glamorous for a second Shelly barely recognised her as she crossed the intensive care unit, but on closer inspection the last twenty-four hours had left their mark, dark hollows surrounding her eyes, lines grooved in her cheeks, and her hands were shaking as she reached out and touched Matthew.

'I'm so sorry,' Marlene sobbed as Ken hovered, wringing his hands in despair. 'So sorry we weren't here for you. How is he? Ross said he was picking up a bit.'

'Ross?'

Marlene was dabbing at her eyes as she looked down at Matthew. 'He picked us up from the airport and drove us straight here. We had no idea who he was, of course. He was holding up a sign with our names on!'

'He's one of the doctors here.'

Marlene nodded, her glassy eyes straying to Matthew. 'He said he'd been helping you out with the babysitting. Oh, Shelly we should never have gone, never left you—'

'Mum,' Shelly broke in. 'It would have happened anyway.' But though she said all the right things, though she comforted her mother, Shelly's mind was whirring. So wrapped up in herself and Matthew it had never entered her head how Marlene and Ken would get from the airport, never even thought about the angst-filled taxi ride battling peak-hour traffic as they struggled to get to the hospital.

But Ross had.

'He's stabilised, they've stopped all anticonvulsants.' She watched Marlene frown, the medical terminology that came so easily to Shelly lost on Marlene. 'He hasn't had any more fits so they're weaning him off the medication, and the antibiotics seem to have kicked in. They're going to try and get him off the ventilator tomorrow.' Shelly swallowed hard, hating to douse the water on Marlene's hope. 'We won't know for a while yet if there's been any lasting damage.'

'You mean brain damage,' Marlene gasped as she started to cry again, but, catching Shelly's strained face, Marlene checked herself. 'I'm sorry, Shelly, I'm supposed to be being strong for you.'

'I know, Mum, but it's not that easy, is it?'

Julie came off the stool then. It was long into her third shift with Matthew, watching Shelly dozing fitfully on a chair by the bed, and she finally put her foot down.

'How about letting your mum and dad have some time with him, and you go and get some sleep, some proper sleep?' she said as Shelly shook her head. 'And I'm not taking no for an answer this time. You're going to end up being admitted with exhaustion if you don't get some rest.'

'She's right.' Marlene's insistence, combined with Julie's, was more than Shelly could argue with, and now her parents were finally here Shelly felt herself able to hand over the reins a touch, to finally let down her guard a fraction.

'You'll call me,' Shelly checked.

'In a flash.'

A small, plastic-mattressed bed had never looked more inviting. For once Shelly didn't bother tucking in corners, turning back blankets. Instead, she threw on the pillow case and a bottom sheet and stretched out, pulling the white hospital blanket over her. The last time she had lain down she had been holding Matthew, so blissfully oblivious of the impending disaster, so completely unaware how fate was about to roll the dice and throw up another challenge for her to deal with.

Her mind clicked backwards, reliving the precious hours beforehand when for a short while at least the world had been gentler, kindlier, easier.

When she had lain in Ross's arms…

'Shelly.' For a second or two fantasy met reality. A lazy second where the face filling her dreams was really here, where a strong hand was gently touching her arm. 'Shelly.' Her shoulder was being shaken now, dragging her out of her long slumber away from the bliss of a long-awaited sleep.

'What happened?' Sitting bolt upright, Shelly's eyes flashed open, taking in Ross sitting on the edge of her bed, his face now cleanly shaven, his eyes void of their usual easy welcoming smile. 'What's wrong?'

'Nothing,' Ross said quickly, pushing her gently back onto the pillow. 'He's actually picking up, but I just needed to talk to you for a moment.'

She lay back down, allowing the world to come more slowly into focus, listening as Ross spoke, acutely aware of her unmade-up face and unkempt hair, so drab in comparison to a well-groomed Ross.

'They're going to give him a trial without the ventilator tonight. Your mum's with him.' His hand gently held her down as Shelly's first instinct was to rush back to Matthew. 'And what I've got to say won't take a moment.'

She owed him a moment, Shelly knew that much. Whatever had gone on between them, Ross had been wonderful where Matthew had been concerned. 'Dr Khan thinks if he improves enough overnight they might even send him over to the children's ward tomorrow or the next day.'

'So soon?'

Ross nodded. 'Which means I'll be looking after him.' He watched her face as he spoke. 'If you've got a problem with that, tell me now, Shelly. If I tell Dr Khan now, at least we'll be able to arrange something.'

'Why wouldn't I want you looking after him?' Shelly asked bemused as Ross gave a hollow laugh.

'It's my fault he's here in the first place.'

Shelly shook her head, floored by what he was saying. 'Ross, I'm a nurse, I work on a children's ward, I was there when you examined him, this is no one's fault.'

He gave a brief nod, but she could almost feel the self-doubt churning in his usually confident mind.

'What about what's happened between us?'

'Ross.' Shelly's voice so soft he had to strain to catch it. 'That's no one's fault either, it's just something that can never be...' Uncoiling her long legs, Shelly put her bare feet on the floor. 'I need to go to him.'

'Sure.'

Slipping on her sandals, she made for the door, expecting Ross to get up and follow her. Instead, he stayed sitting on the bed, not watching her, not watching anything, just staring at the bland cream wall. 'Are you coming?'

Ross gave a brief nod but made no attempt to move. 'I'll be out in a minute. I'll catch you on the ward, then?' He held up both hands. 'Fingers crossed.'

Holding up her own crossed fingers, Shelly managed a watery smile. 'Fingers crossed,' she murmured, before quietly closing the door behind her.

With Julie's intervention, they let Shelly stay as Matthew was extubated, but even though it went well, even though he breathed on his own, holding his oxygen saturations with just an oxygen mask, Shelly felt a pang of guilt as a sense of anticlimax washed over her.

For three days and two long, long nights she had prayed for this moment, but in her dreams Matthew had opened his eyes, looked right at her. Instead, he just lay there, and Shelly, if there had ever been any doubt, realised then that this was only the beginning of a long exhausting journey. That the Matthew she had kissed goodnight on Thursday would, at best, return to her only in stages, that the deluge of questions about brain damage and long-term effects wasn't going to be answered in the next few days. It was a matter of wait and see, two steps forward one step backwards, and no amount of questions or tests were going to give Shelly a conclusive answer.

The night seemed to go on for ever. Matthew's consciousness level lightened but there was no joyous reunion, just a teary little boy, uncomfortable, pulling at the tubes, staring blankly at a concerned Shelly who did her best to comfort him, to pull him back to her. And despite the presence of her parents, the level of care delivered, Shelly ached, physically ached, for the presence of Ross, for a partner who would willingly share the load, for that mind-reader who instinctively seemed to know how she was feeling. When Dr Khan did the ward round and agreed Matthew could be moved over to the children's ward, Shelly wrestled with the surge of relief that filled her, the knowledge Ross would now be near, reminding herself she had chosen to go it alone.

She was greeted like a long-lost friend on the children's ward, even Tania, reserved to say the least, managed a welcoming smile and a quick pat on her arm.

'Anything we can do to make things easier for you, Shelly, you just have to say. You know where the kitchen is!'

Shelly suppressed an out-of-place smile. The kitchen on the children's ward was hallowed territory indeed, way out of bounds for the parents of patients, and Tania allowing her to use it was a concession indeed!

'Thanks, Tania, and I'm sorry for all the trouble with the roster.'

'Don't even give it a thought. When Matthew improves we'll have a chat, try and work something out. Now, we've put Matthew in a side room, not because he's infectious but the noise on the ward will make him irritable. It might be better to keep the curtains closed if he's still a bit sensitive to light. Still, don't be a prisoner, you can have the door open whenever you want—he's not in isolation.'

The small side room that Shelly knew so well was amazingly unfamiliar with Matthew lying on the bed. Shelly unpacked her bag, then sat awkwardly on the bed, trying to read the nursing charts from her upside-down stance, trying to see what had been written about Matthew, listening to the happy chatter of the ward outside, the hustle and bustle she was so used to being a part of.

'Only me.' Ross gave a brief knock on the open door as Shelly stood up abruptly. 'I've got to admit him.'

'Sure.'

'I know you've answered all these questions a hundred times, but now he's under the care of the ward we have to go through it all over again.'

'Of course,' Shelly said brightly, her voice coming out way too loud as she struggled not to show how awkward she was feeling.

Ross pulled up a couple of chairs and gestured for her to sit down. Even her legs didn't seem to know how to behave as Shelly crossed them too high then shifted uncomfortably as Ross opened the notes.

'I know most of it already, so it shouldn't take too long.'

Five minutes would have been too long in Shelly's highly anxious state. Trying to remember immunisation dates and Matthew's milestones was worse than sitting her high school exams as Ross sat patiently awaiting her answers. She hated the awkwardness between them, the attempt at being professional, the distance she had insisted upon.

'Ross!' Nicola, the student, back on days now, was smiling at the door. 'Hi, Shelly, sorry to hear about Matthew.' She turned back to Ross her colour deepening as she spoke. 'Tania wants to know when you'll be able to review cot four.'

'Tell her I won't be long.' Ross barely looked up. He probably didn't even notice the breathlessness in Nicola's voice, the reddened cheeks. Ross probably thought the entire female population were created two shades pinker with fluttering eyelashes, such was his effect on women. Standing up, he made his way over to the bed and examined a sleeping Matthew gently. 'Has he spoken at all yet?'

'Nothing,' Shelly said, hovering anxiously. 'He's just grizzling sometimes and pulling at everything.'

Ross nodded thoughtfully. 'He's still got meningitis, Shelly. Just because he's out of Intensive Care, it doesn't mean he's over it.

He's still fighting a massive infection, and very sick, so don't be alarmed that he's not responding to you.'

'I know,' Shelly said, then gave a tired smile. 'Actually, I don't. It's hard to be objective when it's your own child.'

'Of course it is.' There was a horrible awkward pause and Shelly so wanted to speak, so wanted to fill it, but she truly didn't know what to say. 'I'd better get on.'

Despite Tania's invitation to keep the door open, Shelly closed it gently behind him and in the days that followed more often than not that was the way it stayed. Far, far easier to shut herself away, to block out the noise of the world around her, than to hear him, to see him and know she couldn't have him.

Visitors were exhausting, and as much as Shelly was grateful for them coming, for caring, she was always relieved when they left. Even Marlene seemed draining. The only person Shelly actually looked forward to seeing was Melissa. Under her quiet charge Shelly slept easily, crawling on the bed beside Matthew, knowing they were in good hands, welcoming the contraband coffee Melissa bought into her room each morning.

'Remember to take the cup out,' Melissa warned, 'or Tania will have a fit.

'So are you ready for the off?'

Rubbing her eyes, Shelly crept quietly out of bed, anxious not to wake Matthew and enjoy her five minutes' peace. 'Can you believe I'm nervous?'

'Of course you are,' Melissa said wisely. 'But you're going to be fine. Once he's back home you'll soon see a huge improvement.'

'There already is.' Shelly looked over at the bed. 'It's hard to believe just a week ago he was in Intensive Care. Now just look at him, demanding the television on. He walked a couple of steps yesterday, you know.'

'I know.' Melissa smiled. 'And he'll no doubt walk a few more today. Just take it slowly, and don't expect too much too soon, and he'll get there.' She paused for a second, her voice lowering a touch as she looked Shelly square in the eye. 'I'm not so sure about you, though.'

'Me?' Shelly checked, giving Melissa a wide-eyed look.

'Yes, you. Holed up in here, barely putting your head out of the door. You can't avoid Ross for ever.'

'I'm not trying to avoid him,' Shelly said quickly. 'I just needed some time out and, believe it or not, it's actually been quite nice being cooped up in here. For once in my life I've had some time to think things through, make a few decisions of my own.'

'Such as?'

'I'm handing in my notice.' She watched as Melissa frowned but Shelly shook her head. 'It has nothing to do with Ross. I don't want Matthew going back to crèche. I've nothing against it, I'm sure it's done him wonders, but I'm going to be a stay-at-home mum.'

'How will you afford it?'

Shelly held up the calculator she had on the bedside table. 'Another thing I've been doing while I've been cooped up in here. I won't be that much worse off. The crèche fees are huge, and if I can do the odd casual shift at weekends we'll just about break even.' Shelly grimaced.

'So long as the car stays healthy and the air-conditioner doesn't finally give in and die on me. But, either way, it's something I have to do, Melissa, we'll have to make do with what we've got. I just want Matthew to enjoy his childhood his way, not Neil's, not Mum's, just his. I'm not giving up on him, I'll do my best but I'm just tired of him being pushed every which way.'

'Fair enough,' Melissa said slowly. 'So long as you're not handing your notice in because of Ross.'

'I'm not that stupid.'

'Good.' Melissa stood up and took Shelly's drained cup. 'But just in case Ross does factor into this little life plan you've just suddenly come up with, you'd best know that Ross has handed his own notice in this week.' She watched as Shelly struggled to look impassive. 'He's going back to the outback, to work at that darned clinic he's always going on about.

'You don't look very surprised. Had he already told you?'

Shelly forced a half-smile. 'We're a bit beyond the confiding-in-each-other stage, we barely manage a good morning. No, the reason I'm not surprised is because deep down I knew all along he wasn't going to be here for ever, and I guess this kind of proves me right.'

'What went wrong, Shelly?' There was nothing nosy in Melissa's question, just genuine concern. 'You two just seemed so right for each other.'

'We are.' Shelly smiled at Melissa's confusion. 'And no doubt in another place, another time we'd have had the best relationship, but it just can't be. We're just too different.'

'But if you love each other, surely you can work things out.'

Shelly shook her head sadly. 'Look at you and Dr Khan. You knew it was over before you even started.'

'That was different,' Melissa argued. 'Mushi had his culture, his family.'

'I've got a son,' Shelly said firmly. 'A son with special needs. Ross is young, carefree, and with the whole world ahead of him it just couldn't work.

'It couldn't,' Shelly insisted as Melissa opened her mouth to argue. 'How can I land all this on Ross? It was hard enough before the meningitis but no one can tell if there's going to be any long-term damage. It's hard enough for me to deal with, let alone anyone else. Even Matthew's own father doesn't…' Shelly stopped talking as Matthew stirred. She knew he didn't understand what was being said, but the words were too cruel to be spoken in his presence. 'It's better we realise that now than in a few months' or years' time when Matthew's devoted to him. I'm not going to let Matthew be hurt again.'

'What about you?' Melissa questioned. 'What about your needs?'

'I'm fine,' Shelly said firmly. 'I've got everything I need right here.' Walking over to the bedside, she smiled as Matthew opened his eyes and gazed up at her, his little face breaking into a smile as he lifted his arms to be picked up. 'Haven't I, darling?'

'It's good to be home.' Turning the key in the lock, Shelly smiled at her mother as she stepped inside. The house was back to its usual spotless self, the carpets freshly vacuumed, the kitchen spotless. Carrying a sleeping Matthew through to his room, Shelly noticed the fresh sheets on the bed, not a single shred of evidence to indicate the awful event that had unfolded the last time she had been here.

'You've been busy,' Shelly said, laying Matthew down on the bed.

'I haven't even set foot in the place,' Marlene corrected, bustling around, pulling curtains and tucking a duvet around the sleeping child. 'That Ross said he was going to pop around and pick up his stuff. He must have had a tidy up. You should make a bit of effort with him, you know, Shelly. It's not every day you find a man who comes house-trained.'

Shelly smothered a smile as she popped a kiss on Matthew's cheek and left him to sleep.

Ross was hardly house-trained. He'd probably hired someone to do the work.

Still…

Looking around at the spotless house, in that second Shelly would have given anything to have it back to the chaos Ross so easily generated. For a pile of newspapers to litter the benches, for his grubby old sleeping bag to be thrown over the sofa, for the inevitable take-away boxes to be spilling over the sides of the bin.

'Why don't you go and lie down?' Marlene suggested. 'While Matthew's asleep. You look completely done in.'

Shelly didn't need to be asked twice. The euphoria of Matthew coming home was tempered with a weary exhaustion. The ten days he had spent in the hospital had seemed more like a month.

Not quite house-trained. Shelly smiled as she stretched out on the bed. Ross's domestic duties hadn't stretched to making *her* bed and as she snuggled into the pillow the scent of his aftershave washed over her, a delicious, painful taste of all she had had, all she had let go.

CHAPTER TWELVE

'HOW'S Matthew?'

Everyone was asking—Dr Khan as Shelly turned into the corridor, the domestic mopping the floor as Shelly walked onto the ward. Even Tania managed a rather twisted attempt at a smile as Shelly walked onto the ward for the first time in a fortnight.

'Getting there,' Shelly repeated for what felt like the hundredth time, the two little words enough for now, enough for a busy morning when work was on the agenda, but Tania was obviously in the mood for a chat. 'Who's looking after him while you're working?'

'Mum and Dad. He's not well enough to go to crèche.'

'Time for a quick chat?' Tania never chatted and with a sinking heart Shelly followed her into the office. Her first day back and Shelly felt as nervous as she had when she had just qualified, Matthew's illness having taken its toll on her own confidence. Still, Shelly consoled herself as she made her way to Tania's office, bracing herself for another plea to reconsider her notice. Only two weeks to go and she would be taking care of her own child at long last, and no amount of cajoling from Tania was going to make her change her mind!

'We had an admission last night.' Tania gestured for Shelly to sit down. 'I wanted to talk to you before you heard it at handover.'

Frowning, Shelly sat down, her frown deepening as Tania continued.

'Angus Marshall, a twenty-month-old…'

'I know the one,' Shelly interrupted. 'So what happened?'

'He "fell" again.'

Shelly heard the quotation marks around the word and held her breath as Tania continued. 'He's got a head injury. Thankfully it's not too serious, but he's been admitted so that Community Services can get involved.'

'They should have been involved last admission,' Shelly retorted, not caring that this was her senior she was addressing, angry and bitter that her observations and concerns had been dismissed, angry that even with Ross's intervention Angus had been allowed to go home for it all to happen again.

'I know you had your suspicions about Angus. Melissa and Ross did, too, but at the time there wasn't enough to go on. Children have accidents. We can't point the finger of accusation based on hunches. The Marshalls' stories corroborated the injury, there was no previous history and nothing on the child to suggest he was anything other than loved and cared for. We still don't know that that isn't the case. Accidents don't always happen once. He may have fallen again but, given his history we'll be investigating.'

'It should have been done last time,' Shelly argued, refusing to back down. 'I know I'm not particularly senior but Melissa is a charge nurse, Ross is a doctor.'

'Shelly,' Tania snapped, 'out there on this ward there's probably another child slipping through the net as we speak and, as abhorrent as that thought is, it doesn't mean that we're not doing our job properly. Child abuse is an insidious disease that doesn't always manifest itself clearly. We can only go on the evidence we have, and in Angus's case frankly we didn't have enough.

'Now, I've called you in here the same way I've called Melissa in, because this type of conversation is better to have away from handover. We've got students and grads and I don't want them treating the Marshalls differently. Of course they have to know that Angus is a child at risk but any steam that needs to blown off is to be done in here, do you understand that?'

Shelly took a deep breath and gave a reluctant nod.

'Now, you'll be pleased to know that Melissa's on days for a while. I've already spoken to her about it, so when you go out there make sure that it's business as usual, please, Shelly.'

Melissa's rolling eyes as Shelly entered handover left Shelly in no doubt she'd just been privy to the same little lecture. The mood in handover was as volatile as ever, particularly when Melissa pulled rank over Annie and delegated the staff to their patients.

'Shelly cots one to four. Ross needs to admit Angus and no doubt Dr Khan will want to be there, but I'll sit in on that interview, it might be better if you just concentrate on nursing Angus.'

'Fine.' Shelly scribbled a few details on her notebook. Normally she would have been present while her patient was admitted, but in sensitive situations like this Melissa was right to pull her away. Undoubtedly the parents would be upset and defensive and the last thing needed was an atmosphere around Angus. If Shelly could distance herself from the investigative side of things, it would make it easier for the Marshalls to relate to her, make it easier for normality to prevail around Angus.

Heading out onto the ward, Melissa caught up. 'Business as usual,' she muttered. 'Tania's little lecture reminded me why I prefer nights.'

'Tell me about it,' Shelly mumbled.

But no matter how she felt internally, Tania's words were the order of the day. Smiling brightly, business as usual resumed as Shelly walked into the room. 'Good morning, Mrs Marshall,' she said, then made her way over to Angus, who was resting quietly in his cot. 'How's Angus?'

'Tired,' Mrs Marshall said, her eyes red-rimmed, her voice shaky. 'We were in Emergency all night, we've only been on the ward for an hour.'

'You must be exhausted,' Shelly said sympathetically. 'I won't open up the curtains, then, I'll just do Angus's obs and then we'll let him rest. He can have a bath a bit later on.'

'The night sister said the doctor will be along to admit him soon.'

'That's right, Dr Bodey's on this morning, it mightn't be for a while yet, though as I think he's still stuck in Emergency. Why don't you lie down and have a rest? We'll wake you when he comes.'

Mrs Marshall nodded and sat wearily down on the camp bed. 'I wonder how Doug's going?'

'You've got two others, haven't you?'

Mrs Marshall nodded. 'The older one will be going to school soon. Doug's going to come by then.'

'Good.'

Shelly didn't say much more, just busied herself doing the obs, and her wooden movements had nothing to do with the rather awkward situation. Instead, she felt like a complete novice. Everything felt new and unfamiliar and every shred of her wanted to be at home with Matthew.

Her other three patients were relatively well. A couple of the babies had bronchiolitis but had long since turned the corner and Shelly spent the early part of her shift helping the mums bath them, mindful of their drips and oxygen and doing their obs. Her other charge, Timmy Dale, was on his way to Theatre for a circumcision and the only thing on his little mind was when he was going to get his breakfast!

'Shouldn't be too long now,' Shelly said hopefully to Timmy's anxious mother.

'He wants a bottle.'

'The babies are put at the beginning of the theatre list for that very reason.' Shelly grinned, offering to hold him while his mum nipped out for a coffee. 'I'll call you if the porters come.'

Shelly felt herself stiffen as through the glass she saw an anxious-looking man walk into Angus's room and Mrs Marshall jump up to greet him. The glass wasn't thin enough to allow her to hear what was being said but from the looks on their faces they weren't greeting each other particularly fondly. 'I'll go.' Melissa popped her head in as Shelly attempted to put a wailing Timmy back in his cot. 'Ross and Dr Khan are here now anyway, we may as well get this over with now. How was she with you?'

'Fine,' Shelly replied. 'I don't know whether or not she realises we're suspicious.'

'Well, she's about to find out.'

A brief glimpse of the back of Ross's head was all Shelly gleaned, but it was enough to throw her into turmoil. But there wasn't any time for introspection, not when the porters were bearing down and Timmy was ready to be wheeled off to Theatre.

Taking him across, Shelly kept up with the porters' light-hearted chatter, handed over her little charge to the theatre staff, even managed to find a box of tissues for Mrs Dale when it all became too much, and for all the world not one person would have guessed she was operating on autopilot, functioning with a broken heart.

'So, is it good to be back?'

Shelly started slightly when Ross came into the coffee-room but recovered quickly.

'No,' she admitted. 'But it's only for a couple of weeks.'

'I heard.' His polite answer was almost dismissive and Shelly gave a small shrug and turned back to her magazine, frowning. She had expected a bit of discomfort between them on her return but Ross seemed a million miles away and not remotely bothered that she was here as he spooned coffee and sugar into his cup and paced around, waiting for the ancient old kettle to boil.

'How's Matthew?' This Shelly had braced herself for, and even though she had decided Ross deserved a bit more than her customary answer, from the forced concentration on his face, his obvious distraction, Shelly took her usual option.

'Getting there.'

'Good.'

Picking up a paper, he started to read it but the insistent tapping of his foot told Shelly he wasn't taking anything in.

'Are you all right, Ross?' Shelly ventured, ducking behind her magazine when Ross gave an irritated sigh.

'Never been better,' he snapped, and Shelly stood up and drained her cup, grateful for the excuse to end this difficult meeting.

'Well, if you've finished interviewing the Marshalls, I'd better get back out there,' she said.

'*They* haven't finished yet, so you can take your time with your coffee.' He was almost snapping and, bemused, Shelly sat back down. 'Melissa and Dr Khan did their usual double act,' he explained. 'She suddenly remembered a drug chart I needed to write and he followed me out, then told me to wait for him in here.'

'Why?'

'Apparently my stance was "too judgmental".' Ross shot her a withering look. 'I'm supposed to sit there like a grinning idiot while I listen to the two of them lie through their teeth.'

'I know it's hard,' Shelly ventured. 'But it's important not to go in there with a formed opinion—'

'Save it, Shelly.' Ross turned back to his paper. 'I don't need a lecture from you of all people.'

She was saved from responding as a furious Melissa appeared at the door. 'Thanks a lot, Ross.'

'Any time,' he snapped, his eyes just as angry as Melissa's.

'You can't be so accusatory. It's not your place. We have to let them give their version of events first, not sit there with arms folded, staring the man down.'

'He's lying,' Ross insisted.

'Probably.' Melissa pushed the door closed. 'But your heavy-handed methods aren't helping matters.'

'What about his heavy hands?' Ross stood up, and Shelly was shocked to see a flash of tears in his eyes. 'And as for my methods, if Dr Khan had listened to me in the first place

Angus wouldn't be lying there with a lump on his head the size of an egg.'

'Ross.' Melissa's voice was calmer now, her anger fading as she responded to the genuine anguish in Ross's voice. 'We don't know all the circumstances, and we're not going to know unless we tread gently. We're not just here for Angus, we're here for the whole family. I've been nursing a long time and I've learnt that things are never clear-cut, particularly in cases like this. Who knows what the dynamics are in place there, what the reasons behind his actions are? Mr Marshall may have been abused himself...'

'That's not a reason,' he growled. 'That's an excuse, and you'll never convince me otherwise.' Ross's usually relaxed face was livid now. 'You really think you know everything, don't you, Melissa? Well, let me tell you here and now that you don't. This place makes me sick.' Wrenching open the door, he stormed outside, leaving a stunned Melissa and Shelly in his wake.

'What,' said Melissa, folding her arms and puffing up her chest, 'is that man's problem?'

'I'm not sure,' Shelly said quietly, standing up and rinsing out her cup, defying her instinct to rush out behind him, to comfort him the way he had so many times comforted her.

'Well, I'd better tell Dr Khan to tread gently. With the mood Ross is in, he might just take his backpack and head off to the bush tonight, and where will that leave us?'

It was hard to carry on as normal. The atmosphere on the ward was awful, Ross furiously writing up his notes as Melissa rubbed everyone up the wrong way.

'She needs a man,' Annie moaned when Shelly met her in the kitchen and they made up a pile of bottles between them.

'She needs a holiday,' Shelly said tactfully. 'We all do.'

'What lunch-break do you want?'

Shelly shrugged. 'The Marshalls are in with the social worker so I'm just going to feed Angus his then I'll probably head off. Can you keep an eye on him for me?'

'Sure, and how's the post-op?'

'About to have his long-awaited bottle.' Shelly held it up. 'And then hopefully a big wee and then home sweet home.'

Angus was lying quietly, staring up at the ceiling, his little face barely turning when Shelly came in and pulled on a gown.

'Hey, Angus, how about some lunch?' Sitting him in his high chair was out of the question with his leg still in plaster, so instead Shelly propped him up in his cot, pulling down the side so she could chat to him while he ate, watching as he tucked into his lunch with gusto.

'Not a big talker, huh?' Shelly smiled as Angus ate on, occasionally shyly looking up at her as she rattled on about teddies and toys and trains and all the things toddlers hold dear. 'That's all right, I can do enough talking for the two of us.'

'Tell me about it.' Ross walked in, an almost shy look on his face, smiling gently at Angus before turning his eyes to her. 'Sorry about earlier.'

'Don't be,' Shelly said easily. 'It gets to all of us, even Melissa, believe it or not.'

'I know.'

'How did it go with Dr Khan?' Shelly asked.

'Good and bad. He gave me a bit of a dressing-down, but I hadn't actually done anything wrong. He was more concerned that I was *going* to say something inappropriate, that's why he got Melissa to get me out.'

'So no harm done, then.' Shelly smiled, wiping a streak of egg off Angus's face, her smile fading as Ross carried on talking.

'I'm finishing up today, Shelly.'

Aghast, she swung around to face him, but Ross was already walking off and because it was a children's ward, because there was a toddler finishing his lunch and cot sides to be put up, Shelly wasn't in any position to follow him.

'Why?' she asked when finally she caught up with him in the doctors' room, ploughing through his notes, his pen working furiously across the paper. 'Why would you leave just like that? We all have our bad days. Dr Khan—'

'Dr Khan has nothing to do with it. Sure, I was out of line so he put me in my place—enough said. I'm not leaving because of that.'

'Because of me,' Shelly ventured as Ross just looked at her. 'But I've only got another two weeks.'

'Because of me,' Ross said simply. 'This place just isn't me, Shelly, and today proved it.'

'So you're running off?'

'Nobody's running,' Ross said, turning back to his notes.

'You know the mess this will leave the staff in.'

'They'll manage,' Ross shrugged. 'They'll get a locum.'

'I was right all along, wasn't I?' Shelly gave a rueful hollow laugh. 'Though I never thought you'd just turn your back like that. I thought that even *you* were a bit more responsible.'

'Well, obviously I'm not.' Ross leant back in his chair. 'So you can pat yourself on your back about your lucky escape, Shelly. You've been waiting for me to show my true colours so you can justify dumping me, well, here they are.' He held up his hands. 'Ross the drifter does it again.'

'I don't get you, Ross.' Shelly shook her head, tears terribly close but she bit them back, determined not to cry. 'I'm leaving so there won't be any awkwardness. You've got so many friends here, a job, a life, and yet you can walk away from it all with just a quick goodbye.'

'Not even that.' Ross stood up and slammed the file he was writing in shut. 'I'm tired of goodbyes.'

'Where will you go?' Shelly sneered, biting back tears, appalled not just at the end of their romance but the terrible, terrible conclusion to their friendship. 'What continent haven't you discovered yet?'

'I'm going home, Shelly.' He clicked his pen off and slipped it into his pocket.

'And where's home this week? What country are you going to bestow yourself on this time, endear yourself to, until the going gets too tough or there's a *policy* that doesn't quite sit right with you?' A heavy dose of sarcasm laced her voice but it disappeared as Ross caught her eye and she saw the pain etched in his features.

'Tennagarrah,' Ross said quietly, his voice a contrast to Shelly's accusatory tones. 'It's the one place on God's earth I've ever really felt I belonged.' He paused at the door, his voice so quiet she could hardly hear it. 'Except for a few nights at your place.'

CHAPTER THIRTEEN

'HOW was work, darling?'

'Don't ask,' Shelly groaned, peeling off her shoes and collapsing onto the sofa as Matthew clambered over her.

'Leave Mummy, darling, until she's had her shower,' Marlene said, casting an anxious look in her daughter's direction and picking Matthew up. But Shelly just laughed.

'He's fine, Mum. He just spent a week on the children's ward, including a few rounds in the playroom, and didn't even catch a cold. I think I've been being a bit precious.'

'My goodness.' Marlene grinned, kissing Matthew. 'Don't be fooled, darling. It might look like Mummy, might even talk like Mummy, but this laid-back woman lying on the sofa is an impostor!'

'Stop.' Shelly grinned. 'You'll give him nightmares.'

'Nothing could upset this gorgeous boy,' Marlene enthused, tickling him as she spoke, obviously delighted to be with him. 'We've had a lovely day. We've made jam tarts and we've read his book, oh, must be a hundred times now. It's amazing, isn't it, how sick he's been and just look at him now.'

'Kids are like that.' Shelly smiled, holding out her arms for a cuddle. 'One minute they're so sick all you can do is pray then suddenly they turn the corner and they're off. Not like adults. We take for ever to get over things.'

'Still,' Marlene mused, 'he's done very well. All the trauma he's been through and he just keeps right on smiling.'

Shelly looked down at Matthew fondly. Marlene was right. She had braced herself for tantrums and long unsettled nights, but Matthew seemed totally content to slip back into his usual routine.

'He must feel secure,' Marlene said fondly. 'That must be it.'

A lump filled in Shelly's throat. For all the crèche, divorce, for all the tumultuous two years they had spent, Matthew did feel secure. She was definitely doing something right.

'He's happy to be home…' Marlene carried on nattering, but Shelly just sat there, staring at Matthew, a million jumbled thoughts tossing in her brain and landing as one, a clear picture forming, so awful so horrible, Shelly could barely even look.

'Mum.'

Marlene stopped mid-flow, the anguish in Shelly's single word speaking volumes.

'What is it, darling? Whatever's wrong?'

On legs that were shaking, Shelly stood up and handed Matthew to Marlene. 'Can you look after him for me?'

'Of course,' Marlene answered, confused, following Shelly out of the lounge as she grabbed her car keys. 'But where on earth are you going?'

'Hopefully to put things right,' Shelly said, giving Matthew and her a quick kiss before she rushed out into the driveway. Starting the car, she wound down the window as Marlene came over, a worried look on her face.

'How long will you be?'

'A while, I hope.' Shelly looked up at her mother's anxious face. 'I really can't explain things now, Mum, there isn't time.'

'Then you'd better get on,' Marlene said, watching as her organised, meticulous daughter shot out of the driveway, then turning to her grandson.

'That's the first grey hair your mother's ever given me,' Marlene said in a fond voice, wandering back into the house with Matthew hoisted firmly on her hip. 'Hopefully it will be the last.'

Finding the doctors' mess wasn't a problem. Shelly had been there a couple of times for the occasional party, or leaving do, but she certainly hadn't graced the doctors' accommodation and the fact she was still dressed in her uniform had Shelly blushing to her roots as she ran an eye over the rows and rows of mail boxes, hoping Ross's name might jump out of her.

'Can I help you?' One of the female doctors Shelly vaguely knew from Emergency came over, and Shelly found herself stammering as she spoke.

'Oh, hi. Rose, isn't it? I'm trying to find which one's Ross Bodey's room.'

'You and every other woman in the place.' Rose grinned then changed track when she saw Shelly's angst-ridden face.

'I really need to talk to him. Look, I know you probably can't tell me which one it is but can you buzz him?' Shelly gestured to the internal telephone. 'Tell him that I'm down here in the foyer.'

'Don't be daft,' Rose grinned. 'He's in room 202, on the second floor. Good luck,' she called as Shelly darted towards the stairs, mumbling a quick thanks as she climbed them two at a time.

Only at his door did Shelly's nerves truly catch up with her. She had no speech rehearsed, no idea what on earth she was going to say to him, just an urgent, irrepressible need to see him, to put things right, to tell him she finally understood. Screwing her eyes closed, biting hard on her lips, Shelly lifted her hand to knock, almost falling inwards as the door suddenly opened and Ross stood there dressed only in the white boxers with love hearts.

Given they were Shelly's personal favourite, she decided to take it as a good omen.

'Do you always close your eyes when you knock on doors?' Ross gestured for her to come in.

'Nervous habit.' Shelly's rather paltry attempt at humour wasn't even rewarded with a smile.

'What can I do for you?'

Not such a good omen, Shelly thought as Ross greeted her like a shopkeeper. The room was amazingly tidy but, then, it couldn't really be untidy, she realised, as apart from his backpack bulging in the corner, the only personal item left was a pair of jeans and a T-shirt tossed on the stripped bed and the stubby of beer Ross was holding.

'It doesn't take long for you to pack.'

Ross shrugged. 'I'm used to it, remember?' Walking over to the small bar fridge, he pulled out a beer and offered it to Shelly who after a moment's hesitation accepted it, struggling to pull off the bottle top and finally taking a nervous sip.

'Not much of a beer drinker, are you?'

Shelly shook her head. 'Not much of a drinker, full stop.' Still with a mouth as dry as sand, Shelly ventured another taste as Ross knelt down and started fiddling with the straps on his backpack.

'When's your flight?'

'Six a.m.' He carried on fiddling with the beastly backpack and Shelly knew he wasn't going to make this easy for her.

'I'm sorry for the things I said, Ross,' she started nervously. 'For insinuating you were irresponsible…'

'I probably deserved it,' Ross conceded. 'I am kind of bailing out.'

'With good reason, though.' For a second she thought he stiffened but he soon shrugged it off and Shelly carried on staring at his bare back as he wandered around the room, which wasn't exactly a hardship. The sight of Ross's bare back actually made even the icy cold beer palatable.

'I just can't go on working in that place.' Ross finally volunteered a conversation. 'I'd barely been back five minutes before I remembered why I'd left in the first place.' His eyes caught hers then. 'Or at least one of the reasons.'

'Which was?'

'I can't stand passing the buck,' he explained slowly. 'I can't stand handing things over, being a small spoke in a big wheel. What happened with Angus today will barely merit a mention, just another cock-up that will be brushed under the carpet, and I'm sick and tired of it. I want to be accountable, Shelly. I want to make my own mistakes, not apologise for someone else's.'

'And you'll get that in the outback.'

'Tenfold,' Ross said simply. 'Look, I know you probably think I'm overreacting, but what happened with Angus…'

Shelly took a deep breath, her hesitant voice forcing Ross's attention.

'Angus's father hasn't been abusing him.' She read the confusion in his face, saw his mouth open to argue with her, but she beat him to it. 'It was his mum.'

'His mum?'

Shelly nodded slowly. 'Mr Marshall was covering up for her so, yes, I guess he was lying. He just didn't know what else to do.'

'His mum?' Ross asked again, his face paling as the news sank in.

'After you'd gone, Mr Marshall asked if he could have a word. Apparently since the new baby came along, she's changed...'

'Postnatal depression?'

Shelly nodded. 'It seems that way.' She saw the pain etched in his face and ached to comfort him, but knew more had to be said. 'At least there's hope, Ross. With counselling, medication, they're probably going to be all right.'

'Oh, God.' A shaking hand raked his hair. 'I read it all wrong.'

'We all did,' Shelly said gently. 'But you know as well as I do, problems like that are never straightforward. Sometimes it's hard to be objective.'

'It's my job.'

Shelly nodded. 'And you'll learn from this, we all will. Angus is going to be OK, the whole family are. There's still a lot of love there.'

He nodded briefly, but it was loaded with agony and Shelly held her breath, knowing what was coming next was going to hurt her like hell.

'I overreacted, and there's a reason, Shelly. What happened with Angus, well, it was…' He shook his head, his eyes tearing away from hers, and he walked over to the window, staring out of it and taking a deep breath.

'Personal,' Shelly suggested gently, and she watched again as he stiffened. Only this time he didn't shrug it off. This time every muscle in his body stayed taut and strained and Shelly did the only thing she could, the only thing her mind and body told her to do—went over and placed a trembling hand on the rock of his shoulder, nearly weeping but holding it back as Ross gave a slow lonely nod, one hand coming up to claim hers, his eyes gazing unseeingly out of the window.

'How bad was it for you, Ross?' Her voice was trembling as she spoke but she struggled to hold it together, knowing that the only tears in place here were Ross's.

'Bad enough.' Still he didn't look at her but the warmth of his hand tightened around hers. 'Pretty much like Angus, except there wasn't any love there beneath the surface. But just like Angus, no one believed it was possible. My father's a doctor, my mother's a teacher. Two more upstanding citizens you couldn't hope to meet.' He gave a low laugh, utterly void of any humour, and turned to face her. 'I'm not a wanderer, Shelly, I'm not some idle drifter. I've been working and studying since I was sixteen years old. The only difference is my home has been wherever I've lived at the time. When I went to the outback I knew I'd found my real home, though. For the first time in my life I knew where I belonged.'

'So why didn't you stay? I mean, they wanted a commitment from you, why couldn't you give it?'

'I've already told you that.' His eyes were staring into her very soul and Shelly felt a shiver of excitement as he crossed the room.

'I had unfinished business with a certain nurse.'

'I thought you were joking…'

Ross shook his head. 'I'd never been more serious in my life. I've loved you Shelly, loved you,' he repeated, as Shelly gave an incredulous nervous gasp. 'I dragged myself off to Scotland when I found out you were engaged to Neil, drowned my sorrows in China the night you got married, and threw in the best job I've ever had when I heard that you were divorced.'

'You really came back for me?' Shelly gasped, the magnitude of his words starting to hit home.

'In a heartbeat. Shelly, Melissa's great and everything, but do you really think I called her to find out about Tania's varicose vein operation or the latest gossip on the ward? I ploughed my way through it so I could casually ask about you. You,' he said, taking her face in her hands and staring into the glassy pools of her eyes. 'And I'm sorry, so sorry that it isn't going to work. And as much as I hate the fact, I have to respect your decision.'

'What decision?' Shelly croaked, dragging him back as he dropped his hands and reached for his beer. 'I didn't know how you felt, I didn't know what you'd been through.'

'Shelly.' Ross's voice was sharp. 'I'm not what Matthew needs. Those were your words and maybe you're right, I misdiagnosed him, for heaven's sake.' He ignored her frantically shaking head, speaking over her until she had no choice but to listen. 'Maybe Melissa's right. Maybe it is all in the genes. Maybe I don't deserve to be a parent.'

'No, Ross.' Shelly realised then the depths of his suffering, the self-doubts that plagued him, and she ached with the desire to right a thousand wrongs, to unscramble his troubled mind and tell him, show him what a wonderful caring man he was. 'You're going to be a wonderful father, a wonderful loving father, and as for what I said…' Her mind was racing, knowing that what she said now had to be right, had to somehow knock down the barriers of self-doubt Ross had erected, had to somehow reach him before he left her life for ever. 'I love you, too. I think I always have,' she gulped, her eyes blinking as she looked back briefly over the years with the benefit of hindsight. 'I always have,' she said more firmly this time, 'and I'm not proud of that fact. I was married and yet I loved you, and when you breezed back into my life, swept me off my feet and into my bed, it was all too easy and I was scared that one day you were going to grow up, one day you'd look around and realise what a mistake you'd made. That's what I meant when I said that you're not what Matthew needs, nothing else.' Her eyes sparkled with tears as she stood and looked at this beautiful man who had been through so, so much yet somehow had managed to hold it together, somehow had managed to defy all the odds, had made something of himself, had kept right on smiling.

'The silly thing is, you've already grown up, haven't you? You grew up a long, long time ago.'

Ross nodded. 'About twenty years ago.' He gave a half-smile. 'What you see is what you'll get, Shelly—if you still want it.'

'Oh, Ross.' Shelly was trembling as he pulled her towards him. Leaning on his chest, she heard his thumping heart, felt his arms tighten around her, and she clung to him tightly, their bodies in blissful contact, no barriers between them now, the fears that had held them apart gone now, leaving them in warm blissful union.

'Come with me, Shelly,' he whispered. 'We can make a home together.'

Her eyes sprang open, her long lashes brushing his chest as the enormity of what he was saying took shape in her mind, which he read in an instant.

What about Matthew?

'Matthew will be fine.' She hadn't needed to even say it. 'Shelly, they'll accept him there for who he is, wrap their arms around him as they did me. It's the most amazing place in the world and we can be a part of it. He won't be the special needs child, he'll be who he is, Matthew Weaver, or Matthew Bodey, if you'll give me that honour.' The world stopped for a moment. The only sound Shelly could hear was the pounding of her temples as Ross lifted her chin and slowly dragged her eyes to his.

Honour, that one tiny word proving the depth of Ross's love. For so long Shelly had worried that if ever love did come her way then freedom would be the price the man would pay for her love. Yet here was Ross turning everything on its head, saying in that one word that Matthew would never, ever be baggage. That he, Ross Bodey, would be proud to be Matthew's father.

She'd have followed him to the ends of the earth on the strength of that alone.

Her answer was in her kiss, sweet and deep and full of passion. Trembling with desire, they melted onto the floor, mindless of the open curtains and of Marlene waiting anxiously at home. It could all wait for the moment.

'Is that a yes?' Ross mumbled as he fiddled with her name-tag and the endless row of buttons on her blouse.

'How could I say no?' Shelly caught his eye and gave a hint of a wicked smile. 'After all, how many men would stay celibate all those years, pining for little old me?'

Ross gave her a slightly startled look. 'Er, Shelly.' His hands froze mid-button. 'When I said I'd always loved you I meant it, but it doesn't mean...' Looking up, he saw she was laughing and Ross joined in. 'You're a wicked woman, do you know that?'

'Very wicked,' Shelly whispered. The smile was back on his face, the easygoing joking was everything she could have hoped for and more. 'And very, very happy.'

EPILOGUE

'PICKED up any good tips?' Ross spoke over the sound of the engine, bouncing an over-excited Matthew on his knee as the small Cessna barely registered a blip as it tore through the massive blue sky.

Looking up from her survival guide, Shelly grinned. 'If I'm lost in the outback, I can flash my ring at the sun to draw attention to myself.'

'Any excuse to look at that thing,' Ross groaned, as Shelly lifted her hand and admired the huge diamond cluster on her finger.

Six none-too-small diamonds glittered back at her—one, Ross had explained, for every year he had loved her. It was larger than life, ostentatious and the antithesis of what Shelly would have chosen, yet she loved it with a passion.

'It really is in the middle of nowhere, isn't it?' Shelly said, her gaze turning to the window, taking in the endless red of the hot earth, the rock formations so immense, so awe-inspiring Shelly knew the endless books she had read hadn't done them justice. Nothing except the naked eye could appreciate the glorious vastness of the outback and Shelly drank it in, scarcely able to believe that this was going to be home.

Home.

The word bathed her in a glow as warm as the hot Australian sun high in the midday sky, and she stole a look at the two men in her life, two people who had shared a rocky start, yet carried right on smiling. A lump surely as big as Ayers rock seemed to fill her throat as Shelly's gazed lingered, watching one blond and one dark head bent over a book, the ties that bound them now unbreakable, her love strong enough, confident enough for them all.

'The welcoming committee's here.' The thick Aussie accent of Bruce, the pilot, forced her attention and Shelly tore her eyes away, blinking as the ground neared, kicking herself for missing the approach, the first glimpse of her new home. Vast properties, white and brown, were beneath them, a petrol station, a pub, horses. She counted them off as Matthew, sensing Shelly's excitement, strained to get over to her, to see what all the fuss is about.

'Who are all these people?' Shelly asked as the plane bumped down, children, adults running alongside, waving, their mouths grinning, mouthing words they had no chance of hearing as the engine died down.

'Like Bruce said, it's Tennagarrah's welcoming committee.' Ross stood up first, helping Shelly up before handing her Matthew, then impatiently pushing the door and stepping down into a throng of people as Shelly stared in wide-eyed bemusement at Bruce.

'He's a popular guy, that husband of yours.'

'Tell me about it.' Suddenly overcome with shyness, Shelly hovered at the door of the small plane, watching as they greeted Ross with like a long-lost brother, waiting for the curious stares to inevitably come her way.

'Shelly! Matty!' Arms were reaching out to her, a mass of limbs pulling them both into the warm embrace of their new community. Matthew was prised from her and Shelly felt a tiny bubble of alarm rise, sure Matthew would wail in horror at the tactile, overpowering nature of the greeting, but instead he was laughing, giggling, revelling in the moment, one eye fixed on Ross enough to make him feel safe.

The welcome didn't end there. Somehow between the high chatter and laughter Ross managed to carry her over the threshold and, despite the audience and revelry, the look in his eyes as they went through the door made the moment as intimate as it should be, and Shelly was only too happy to be entertained in her own home as she was welcomed the way only Aussies could.

'I think I'm finally getting a taste for beer,' Shelly said with a laugh much later when only a few lingering guests remained hovering around the barbeque outside. Shelly finally made her way in and stood watching Matthew through the flyscreen as he rushed around the veranda with his newfound friends.

'So, what do you think?'

There was a slightly nervous note to Ross's voice as Shelly looked around the vast jarrah-floored lounge, the airy high ceilings, the simple beauty of the furnishings. 'I love it,' she said softly.

'Still worried about being lonely?' Ross tested gently, but Shelly just laughed.

'Hardly. I think I'm going to have to make a booking just to cuddle Matthew at this rate. Anyway, Mum and Dad are coming next month, then after that we've got the honey-mooners...'

'Don't,' Ross said, yelping in mock horror and putting his hands over his ears. 'Melissa and Dr Khan's bedroom will be right on the far side of the house. I don't think I could stand it if I heard the two of them...' He screwed his eyes closed and pulled a face. 'And if she keeps calling him Mushi, I think I'll die of embarrassment.'

'It's lovely.' Shelly laughed, pulling down his hands and making sure they were firmly wrapped around her. 'I think it's just so romantic...'

'Well, you would,' Ross grumbled. 'What gets me is how they managed! All those years of being in love, working alongside each other, and they didn't do a thing about it.'

'He loved his wife,' Shelly explained. 'But somewhere at the back of his heart he loved Melissa, too.'

'But how, how can you let all those years slip by...?' His voice trailed off as he looked at Shelly holding her ring up to him. Another excuse to admire it, if ever she needed one. 'That was a silly question, wasn't it?'

'A very silly question,' Shelly answered, her lips moving towards his, melting at the thought of permanent access to his most divine body. 'And one that I'm not even going to try to answer.'